JENNINGS' WORLD

appeared on the starboard side; all six people stared at the planet in awe. It was beautiful, different from any world in their home system. Where Earth was blue, and Mars red, Jennings' World was a deep, emerald green.

When they had landed and settled themselves in what seemed like a large, empty park, Benarcek heard a rustling noise. Leigh switched on the portable light. A naked man was caught by surprise against the rock wall. He was tall and slender, filthy, covered with mud dried on his arms and legs, leaves and twigs twisted in his beard. He seemed to be about twenty-five to thirty years old, the victim of dietary deficiencies. He raised one hand to his eyes, and stood before them shivering slightly.

"There he is," said Benarcek, his voice full of pity, "our good neighbor across the vast gulf of space." Was this one of the intelligent beings who had sent signals to Earth?

THOSE GENTLE VOICES

A Promethean Romance of the Spaceways

by

GEORGE ALEC EFFINGER

WARNER BOOKS

A Warner Communications Company

WARNER BOOKS EDITION
First Printing: March, 1976

Copyright © 1976 by George Alec Effinger

Cover illustration by Lou Feck

Warner Books, Inc., 75 Rockefeller Plaza, New York, N.Y. 10019

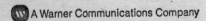 A Warner Communications Company

Printed in the United States of America

Not associated with Warner Press, Inc. of Anderson, Indiana

For Stephan and Julie Cohen, the best double-play combination since Woodie Held and Johnny Temple. They got me out of a tough inning.

... I am not much interested in stories about Martians or 3000 A.D. I have the sort of feeling about fantastic stories that H. G. Wells had: you inject a miracle into a perfectly ordinary setting and then watch the consequences, which are usually bad. The trouble with fantastic fiction as a general rule is the same trouble that afflicts Hungarian playwrights—no third act. The idea and the situation resulting from the idea are fine; but what happens then? How do you turn the corner? ... If a man should wake up in the morning and find that he was nine inches high, I wouldn't be interested in how he got that way but in what he was going to do about it. ...

—Raymond Chandler
In a letter to Hamish Hamilton

PART TWO

1988

CHAPTER 1

It was nearly six weeks into the second International Astrophysical Year. The technicians at the New Orleans Center for Coordinated Astrometrics were still working in a kind of festival atmosphere. The facility had been given a rather large sum of money to pursue chiefly abstract ideas—the sort of assignment these scientists thought of as "fun." Here there were no military contracts, no desperate competition with the world's other interplanetary colonial powers. There was just the opportunity to study the universe with the kind of leisure that had always been necessary, but never practical.

The main building of the New Orleans center was a restored Victorian mansion on St. Charles Avenue. It was shaded by palm trees and surrounded by dense subtropical growth. A long curving drive ran from the avenue up to the pillared front of the great house where, many years before, uniformed servants helped wealthy Orleanians from expensive carriages. Now the old ballrooms were divided into prosaic cubicles for the systems analysts; the several pantries had become the IAY Library Standards Update Center; and, in the back of the lovely old house, overlooking the site of one of old New Orleans's most renowned gardens, a large formal dining room had been cleared of furniture and now housed five of the most sophisticated computers in existence. The 440/65s stood in a row down the middle of the room, beneath the huge, ancient chandeliers. There were two blue 440s, two yellow ones, and one red. At eleven o'clock on the morning of

11

July 9, only the single red console was active. That it was operating at all was a source of concern to the young program analysts in the room.

One young man stood anxiously by the side of a high-speed printout, watching as the computer spewed page after page of indecipherable figures into a wire hopper. Finally, unable to endure the uncertainty any longer, he ripped the pile from the computer, tearing the paper along its perforated edge, and carried the mass of data to his superior, Dr. Janet Short.

"What's wrong, Benarcek?" asked Dr. Short.

"Here," said the technician, "look at this." He dropped the printout sheets on the young woman's desk and waited. She was very busy herself, and this new snag obviously annoyed her. But she pushed her own work aside and paged slowly through the computer's results.

"Where's this coming from? The 440s?" she asked.

"Yes," said Benarcek, "but that's not bad enough. From the red system."

Dr. Short pushed her glasses up, onto the top of her head. Her blue eyes stared at Benarcek for a moment, thoughtfully. Then she roused herself. " It couldn't be," she said at last.

"Well, doggone it, it is," said Benarcek. He stood silently, waiting for Dr. Short's orders.

"Is it still running?" she asked.

"I didn't want to stop it. I can't figure out why it's turning this stuff out, and I was afraid that it would just dump. It was still running when I came in here."

"Okay," said Dr. Short. "Can you bring it in on one of the CRTs?"

"Sure thing, Dr. Short," said Benarcek. He crossed the room to the bank of optical data readers belonging to the Data Retrieval Group. In a few seconds he had plugged into the red system's busy communications, and the strange columns of numbers and equations marched down the green viewscreen of a CRT, just as they had filled the paper pages of the hard-copy printer. Dr. Janet Short watched wordlessly for a full minute.

"Is there a Computer Output Microfilm unit on-line?" she asked.

Benarcek frowned. "I don't think so, Dr. Short," he said. "Just the paper printout."

"Well, can we interrupt this garbage without stopping the whole program?"

"That's what I can't say for sure," said Benarcek, watching the lines of symbols creeping down the face of the CRT. "The red system shouldn't even have gone into operation. Not until the blues and yellows had digested and classified all the Data Source Library programs."

Janet Short stood up and joined the young man by the CRT. She stared at the screen, the emerald glow of the machine casting strange shadows on her youthful features. Her blonde hair was long, tied behind and falling down outside her white lab coat. The unexpected bug in the computer system caused her to frown in concentration, making her look older than her twenty-nine years. "Well, then," she said slowly, perhaps the blues and yellows *are* finished. Maybe this isn't somebody's expensive mistake."

Benarcek shook his head. "It can't be, Dr. Short. We figured on at least three months of documentation before we could even begin the red process. There hasn't been enough time. You saw the books of data. On the short cards it took nearly two weeks to feed it into the blues. Even the new 440s couldn't have correlated it overnight."

"Well, then, our problem is simple," said Dr. Short, switching off the CRT and returning to her desk. "Either this is a basic and pretty stupid error, and we'll have to start all over again; or it's not a mistake, and we'd better be paying attention. The paper printout's still running, isn't it?"

"Yes. Do you want me to stop it?"

"No, no, of course not. We're going to have to analyze these figures. There's a chance these are our results. If they are, somehow we've saved ourselves a couple of months of work." Dr. Short riffled through the pages of printout. "It could be," she said. "It just *could* be."

Benarcek looked doubtful. "The way it's pumping out those figures, it could run all day. If it's garbage, we're going to waste a hell of a lot of computer time. And our budget's mighty small that way, Dr. Short."

She looked up, suddenly very troubled. "You're right.

Okay, I admit I don't know what to do. What do you think?"

Benarcek seemed surprised. "Well, it's certainly over my head. I suppose we ought to let Dr. Jennings know."

"Sure," said Dr. Short with a quick smile. "Grab that stuff and come with me. Maybe if we both pass the buck together it won't look so foolish." Benarcek picked up the folded sheets of computer printout and followed Dr. Short across her office and through the Data Retrieval Resource room, up the wide spiral stairway to the office of Dr. Robert L. Jennings, Jr., chief of the entire astrometrics project. His office had once been the master bedchamber of the mansion, and the thick carpeting and the polished wooden paneling still held tenuous hints of the glory of New Orleans's celebrated Garden District.

Dr. Short stopped outside Jennings's door. She turned to Benarcek, who was standing uncomfortably, shifting the package of computer sheets from arm to arm. Dr. Short smiled encouragingly, but Benarcek only shrugged his shoulders and frowned. The woman turned and knocked loudly on Dr. Jennings's door. There was a long silence, and then the director's secretary came to the door.

"Good morning, Dr. Short," said Miss Brant, the secretary. "Dr. Jennings is on the phone right now. Is your problem serious?"

"I think he's going to have to tell *us* that," said Dr. Short. "I want him to take a look at these results as soon as he possibly can. He might save the project a lot of time and money."

Miss Brant frowned. "I see," she said. "He's talking to IAY Group Two in Washington. But if you think it's important, I'll break in on him. Wait inside, I'll be out in a moment." Miss Brant preceded the two mathematicians across the heavy carpeting of the outer office, knocked briefly on the door of Dr. Jennings's private chamber, and entered. Dr. Short admired Miss Brant's initiative; it was qualities like that that might make the second IAY one of the more important ventures in the history of science. And, at least in the New Orleans center, Dr. Robert L. Jennings, Jr., was personally responsible for the efficiency of his staff.

14

Miss Brant returned quickly. "He cut off his call to Washington," she said. "He'll see you now."

"Thank you, Miss Brant," said Dr. Short. "I think our snag justifies the trouble." Still followed by Benarcek, Janet Short entered the private office of Dr. Jennings, Administrative Director of the New Orleans Center for Coordinated Astrometrics.

Dr. Jennings rose to his full height as he came around his desk to greet them. "Good morning, Dr. Short," he said, reaching to grasp her hand.

"Good morning, Dr. Jennings," said Dr. Short. "Thanks for giving us a minute here. We hit a bug this morning, but a rather strange one. You know Analyst Benarcek, don't you?"

Dr. Jennings smiled and nodded. "Justin has taken me out on his Sunfish a couple of times," he said. Benarcek grinned at the memory. "Now, tell me," said the director, "what kind of bug can make me hang up on the Washington money boys?"

"Well," said Dr. Short, "the whole thing is puzzling. Benarcek, put those sheets down on Dr. Jennings's desk, please." The analyst did so, and Dr. Jennings began idly paging through them.

"Is there something wrong with this data?" he asked.

"I don't really know," said Dr. Short softly. "For all I can tell, they may be perfectly all right. It's more *where* they came from that troubles me."

"All right, Dr. Short," said Jennings, looking at the young woman thoughtfully, "don't have me guessing. Where *did* this garbage come from?"

"The red system," she said.

Dr. Jennings looked very surprised. "That's not what I thought you meant," he said. "Okay, we do have a real dilemma, then. Is there a chance some color-blind operator or programmer pumped up the red instead of the blue machines?" There was an embarrassed silence. "Well," said Dr. Jennings with a short-lived smile, "I was vaguely serious. That kind of foul-up has happened before. I don't suppose anyone's put this stuff through Data Reduction?"

"No, sir," said Benarcek. "It just started coming out

15

a little while ago. I showed it to Dr. Short here, and she figured to show it to you."

"That's the next step, then," said Dr. Jennings. He sat on the corner of his huge mahogany desk and tapped his pen on the pages of data. "While you people downstairs run this through DR, I think I'd better have the EDP Downtime Documentation specialists run some thorough tests on the hardware. And Dr. Short, I expect you'll want your staff to evaluate the whole programming literature. There's been a massive error here, and it'll probably cost us a fortune."

Janet Short frowned. After only six weeks, the "fun" project was already becoming vicious. Dr. Jennings saw her displeasure. "Don't worry," he said. "No heads will roll. There hasn't been any critical sabotage, just a gross waste of time. So let's get back on the track as quickly as possible and try to see that it doesn't happen again."

"Thank you, Dr. Jennings," said Dr. Short. "I sort of feel like the mistakes of those programmers are my responsibility."

Dr. Jennings laughed briefly. "They are, Dr. Short, they are."

Benarcek and Janet Short left the office and retraced the path to their own domain. On the stairs Benarcek spoke up. "You know," he said, "Dr. Jennings is the first director or supervisor I've ever worked under that didn't have a nickname. You know, like 'Ironass' or 'Superwhip' or something like that. Everybody just calls him 'Dr. Jennings'."

"There's a reason for that," said Dr. Short. "I admire the man. I like working for him. I think I want the project to be a success *because* of him. He inspires that kind of cooperation in all of his staff. It's a rare talent."

"That's for sure," said Benarcek.

"So tell me," said Dr. Short as they entered the Data Retrival Group's cubicles, "what's *my* nickname?"

Benarcek just laughed, and Dr. Short pushed him away, smiling. The young supervisor of the Data Retrival Group carried the pages of the printout to her desk She set them down and stared for a few seconds at the severe, military-style walls. She was lost in thought and barely saw her surroundings: a horizontal line at about waist level divided

16

a dark green from the lighter green on all of the walls. Beyond her office, the desks and cubicles cut up the floor space into efficient but unattractive work areas. Overhead, everywhere, were the ugly gray public address loudspeakers. Dr. Short shook her head. What dreams she had entertained in her college days. What romantic visions of gleaming steel and flashing lights. All her training had come down to this, now: a five-pound slab of pure numerical nonsense that had to be sifted for a costly mistake. Just busywork; any high school sophomore could be trained to do it in an hour. But the job itself might take days, even weeks, and the project couldn't afford that. With a sigh, Janet Short sat down at her desk and got to work.

She picked up her phone and dialed the Data Source Library.

"DSL, Miss Briarly," said the voice on the other end.

"Chris," said Dr. Short, "I wonder if you could make up a spare fiche of the Project PTP job material for me."

"*All* of it, Dr. Short?"

"Yes, we found a pretty big bug this morning. We might have to start the whole thing over from scratch. I want all the programs, the variable data addresses, the Job Control Language decks, and the system documentation."

"I'll do my best, Dr. Short," said Miss Briarly skeptically. "How soon do you need all that?"

"Right now."

"Well, you won't have it before tomorrow morning. Can I put it all together? It would be a whole lot simpler that way."

Dr. Short thought for a moment. "Yes, I suppose it *would* be easier for you. But I'm going to have to scan it all on one of these old monoptic readers. You could do me a great favor. Put the program on one fiche, the documentation on another, and the rest of the stuff on a third. And while you're at it, make me a stat of the DSL indexing on Project PTP."

"All right," said Miss Briarly, "but I guess we can't finish all of that before tomorrow night. We'll try, though, Dr. Short."

Dr. Short gritted her teeth. The librarians always knew the easiest way to annoy her. "Good," she said, "try your hardest. Group Two in Washington is going to find out about this before morning, and we're all going to want to be able to reassure them. They have other places to spend their grants, you know."

"I'll have our staff get right to it," said Miss Briarly. From the sudden terseness of the librarian's speech, Dr. Short guessed that the technicians had a talent for annoying the DSL people, as well. Dr. Short sighed as she hung up the phone. She looked at the stack of printout sadly and, rather than tackle it, dialed the phone again.

A man's voice answered. "Data Retrieval Group, Benarcek."

"Janet Short, Justin. Do you have the Data Reduction unit on-line?"

"Check," said Benarcek. "After we left Dr. Jennings's office, I figured that would be the first thing we had to do."

Dr. Short smiled. Her own group was as dependable as any she had ever worked with. If only the semi-skilled jobs could be filled with people with as much interest and concern . . . "Great, Justin. How's it going?"

"Well, we respooled the red system's tapes and fed them through one of the old 1515s that's not being used. The paper tape of the red system's results started spitting out about ten minutes ago, and it's going right into the Data Reduction unit. The 1515 is just reprinting the figures, not computing them; it'll be running about twice as fast as the red system. But the red's got about an hour's head start, and the DR will slow the thing down. I imagine we'll have that stack of paper on your desk reduced by five o'clock tonight. No telling how long the red system'll be putting out new garbage, though. Are you sure you don't want me to stifle it?"

"No, we might as well let it babble. The clue to the whole thing might not show up for quite a while. There's no reason the red system can't stay on until we figure it all out. It's eating up a fortune in computer time, but we can't do anything else in the meantime, anyway."

"All right, Dr. Short," said Benarcek. "Everything in the Group is busily chattering away. All I have to do now is wait. This is going to be one of those jobs where my crossword puzzle talent really gets sharpened up."

Dr. Short muttered a goodbye and hung up. She sighed

18

again. Maybe Benarcek would have nothing better to do than crossword puzzles, but the same could hardly be said for her. She pulled the printout sheets across her desk and reluctantly began her study.

The afternoon passed slowly. After lunch there was a memo on her desk from Dr. Jennings advising her of a supervisors' meeting later in the day. Generally the meetings were long, boring, repetitive, and, because of the guidelines the project received from Group Two in Washington, unavoidable. But the new situation made such a conference necessary; Dr. Short only hoped that by that time someone would have something practical to suggest.

Dr. Short's own work was frustrating; the pages and pages of five-digit numbers meant little to her. After fifteen minutes of sifting the data, she gave up. She would have to wait until Benarcek came in with the Data Reduction profile. She still had to finish some abstracts that she had been writing before the bug appeared. She took up that chore again, but her mind wouldn't concentrate. There was no way that she could understand what was happening within the red system until the technicians finished their tests; she was annoyed that her own routines were so dependent on the others. Still, out of duty she stayed at her desk and wrote reports for the Group Two secretaries to file.

At three-thirty Benarcek came into Dr. Short's office with the DR profile of the first part of the red system's output. "This is that damned bunch of pages we got this morning," he said, putting a small rectangular film on the desk.

Dr. Short picked it up and held it to the fluorescent lights. The fiche was four by six inches, and it held tiny reproductions of forty-nine pages of computer paper printout. Each of those pages represented a decoding and condensing of up to twelve of the original pages that had so baffled Dr. Short.

"Thanks, Justin, for getting it done so quickly," she said. "I can't wait to get at this, but there's a meeting with Dr. Jennings in less than half an hour. By the way, I suppose you ought to make up a fiche for him, too."

"Got it right here," said Benarcek.

"The universe is going to love you, Justin," said Dr. Short. "This project just might stumble on all sorts of tasty things."

"I can just see it in the *A.S.A. Journal:* 'Program Analyst Uncovers Meaning of Life.' It's just waiting here in this fiche, but it'll have to keep. Nothing holds me here past five o'clock, not even the promise of immortality in the halls of Science. I've got tickets for the Indians' game tonight."

Dr. Short laughed. "All right, Justin, you've done your share of work today. Keep that DR going, though; we'll want the whole thing on fiche tomorrow morning. Would you do me a favor before you take that up Dr. Jennings? Would you wheel that old viewer-calculator over to my desk? I want to get at least a glimpse of what our metal friends are trying to pass off as a final answer."

Benarcek did as she asked and left. Dr. Short slipped the fiche into place in the viewer. Instead of columns of five-digit integers, the fiche showed a seemingly endless parade of equations, lists of variables and constant values, analyses of sub-routines, and a running estimate of the margin of error; the latter never seemed to go over eight percent. It would take a while to interpret this data, but it was in a form more readily usable by a human technician. Dr. Short was curious about what Dr. Jennings's reaction might be.

She could not have predicted his excitement accurately. At the meeting of supervisory personnel, he was positively flustered.

"Ladies and gentlemen, let us begin," he said, nodding to Dr. Short as she entered his office, which had been rearranged to accommodate the meeting. "I have here the output of the red system, which Dr. Short's group has partially DRed. I'm going to put this fiche on this screen here, so you all can see it. Now, after just a cursory examination, I've made a few surprising discoveries. First, I don't believe that there's been any kind of major programming error, after all."

The room full of department heads reacted with surprise. "If you mean that," said Dr. Milton Rausch, the project's chief hardware engineer, "you have to mean that we have our answer. It's impossible for the red system to operate until the blue and yellow have completed all the preliminary computations. The only thing that could come out of the red is the final results. And if there isn't any program bug, then . . . uh . . . Project PTP can type up its report and go home."

"Well, not quite," said Dr. Jennings. "The prime objective of Project PTP, simply speaking, is to correlate the astronomical data that has accumulated during the last few decades. Then, by purely mathematical means, we are to ascertain whether any intelligent agency could be responsible for largely unexplained cosmic phenomena discovered since the development of modern astrometric apparatus. It is possible that the answer to that very important puzzle is right here." Dr. Jennings touched the screen on which the fiche was projected. "We'll know for certain very shortly. But even if this facet of our research has so abruptly ended, we are still faced with many weeks of work. There is no reason for concern about your jobs, and you should strive to reassure your subordinates along these lines." The others laughed.

Dr. James Chareaux, the chief of the Standards Update section, spoke up. "I just can't accept it, Bob. I can't see how even the 440/65s could have gone through that data so quickly."

"It's easy, Jim," said Dr. Jennings, with his familiar quiet smile. "All it means is that the answer is a whole lot simpler than we've ever wanted to believe. What information we've been able to gather concerning such things as QS Radio Sources, pulsars, and most especially Orienne-Mallesque stars has done little to illuminate our conception of the universe. In the last twenty-five years, science has stored away few facts and many theories. Now, with the techniques and facilities we have mobilized through the International Astrophysical Year, we're attempting to close in on some of those secrets. We can chart the relative positions and velocities of these phenomena; we can predict with a fair degree of accuracy the sudden appearances and disappearances which so baffled our colleagues twenty years ago. Using hydrogen-line frequency measurements we can estimate the size and age of each anomaly. We all know how long it took to assemble this material, to code it, to fit it all into a massive

21

series of programs digestible by our 440s. We did our job, and the 440s did theirs. We're just about six months ahead of schedule."

"I still don't believe it," said Dr. Chareaux.

"Well, perhaps this morning the universe merely laughed in our faces," said Dr. Jennings, shrugging. "We'll find out."

"The problem doesn't have to be in the software," said Dr. Short. Her voice was softly modulated, a sharp contrast to Dr. Jennings's loud enthusiasm and Dr. Chareaux's persistent doubt. "It may be a simple failure of the machines themselves."

"We spent the afternoon checking them out," said Dr. Rausch. "I'll vouch for the blue and yellow systems. There's not much we can do with the red until it stops its routine, but what we have checked has been perfectly normal."

"Well, gang," said Dr. Jennings, "that's the situation. If I'm correct, and for the sake of my scientific curiosity I hope that I am, we may know tomorrow whether or not the human race is alone in the universe. I feel certain that this data will pinpoint our cosmic neighbors, or once and for all destroy the hope of finding any. Off the record, I'm praying that your analyses will prove me right, that this isn't just the result of some malfunction. There's no need to express how disappointed we'd all be. For that reason alone, I see no cause to advise anyone, neither our superiors in Washington nor outsiders, of the situation until we have something more definite. I'm personally frustrated by the delay, but there's no point in beginning work until the red system has decided that it's finished its job. I hope that will occur sometime tonight. So, if all goes well, in the morning we may be able to divide the computer's output among you, and the second phase of Project PTP will begin. I suggest you all go home, get a good night's rest, and come in with as clear a head as you can manage. I don't suppose I'll have to ask you to be on time." He smiled and indicated that the meeting was over.

Afterward, there was a cluster of people around Dr. Jennings, all anxiously trying to get him to elaborate on the reasons for his optimism, but he would say nothing

22

further. Janet Short was less interested, preferring to wait until the data became definite. She was absorbed in her own thoughts on the way back to her office, when she became aware that Dr. Jennings had spoken to her. She turned to see him following her down the curving staircase.

"You're certainly keeping your own counsel about this, Dr. Short," said the tall, serious, administrative director.

Dr. Short smiled self-consciously. "I don't really see any purpose in putting forth any ideas until I have a chance to study the facts. I haven't even had time to get as familiar with them as you are."

"I suppose yours is the safest and wisest course," said Dr. Jennings, finding in her words an amused reference to his own excitement. "That's why I advised temporary secrecy to the others. But I'm sure you can understand what this project means to me. To have an answer—and to such a question, after all!—nearly within my reach is enough to drive me crazy. I guess I'll have to wait, but I don't have to enjoy it."

They walked together past the security guard at the old mansion's great double doors. The late afternoon sun was still hot, and emerging from the air-conditioned interior onto the columned porch they were halted by the stifling atmosphere.

"I still haven't gotten used to this weather," said Dr. Short, shaking her head ruefully.

"You came from New York, didn't you?" asked Dr. Jennings.

"I'm sure you have my folder memorized by now," said Dr. Short. "And my last job isn't interesting enough to start a real conversation. But I did quite a bit of work in dexterity equivalencies. I had a grant from the Biomath people in St. Louis, along with an old colleague of mine. But, of course, the money ran out just as we were beginning to show some results."

"At least we don't have that problem here," said Dr. Jennings. "It's a very rare circumstance, having administrators in Washington who admit they don't know what's happening and are willing to trust my judgment. They'll

23

gladly pay for any toy I requisition, because they know that basically I'm stingier than they are."

"So far, it's been a real joy working here."

Dr. Jennings smiled. "I'm glad to hear that," he said. "You mean all except this weather, huh?"

"It's not the heat, it's the humidity," she said, laughing.

"Sometimes it's both. Has it kept you from exploring our part of the country?" They left the porch and walked down the drive together.

"When I first got to town, I was told to look into the French Quarter. I went down to Bourbon Street and I was pretty disappointed. All there was were rows of strip joints and bars. It was like the owners were still stuck back in 1970 or something. Nothing different from any big town I've ever seen. New York has Times Square, Baltimore has its Block, Cleveland has its Short Vincent. I guess I just have better ways to spend my time."

"I hope that doesn't mean that you're going to be one of those dedicated scientists, always stuck in a hot room reading journals right through Mardi Gras," said Dr. Jennings.

Dr. Short was taken aback for a few seconds. She didn't want to seem overly prim, but she didn't want to look foolish, either. She was spared the necessity of answering by Dr. Jennings's sudden apology.

"I'm very sorry, Dr. Short," he said softly. "I suppose I got out of line for a minute. I didn't mean to be so accusing. It's just that visitors to New Orleans generally get only a quick glimpse of our city, as you said, just a bit of Bourbon Street's flash and racket. It's frustrating to me, because New Orleans is one of the most fascinating places in the United States, even the world. We natives want it to be properly appreciated."

"Oh, there's no need for you to apologize," said Dr. Short quickly. "I understand perfectly. It's only that sometimes it's more difficult for a newcomer to find the right places."

"Well, then," said Dr. Jennings, "I'd be flattered if you'd let me help you discover some of our more essential sights."

Dr. Short paused on the sidewalk, considering the propriety of the situation, but stopped that line of thought when she looked into her director's pleasant, open face. "Nothing could make me happier," she said, smiling again. "But don't we have to worry about interoffice gossip?"

"They wouldn't dare," said Dr. Jennings. "I'm too easy a target, and you're too fine a person."

"With a line like that," she said, "it's lucky you weren't an English major, Dr. Jennings."

"First off," he said, "we drop the 'Doctors' after five o'clock. I'm Bob and you're Janet. I'll call my waiter and see about a table at Antoine's for dinner."

"That would be wonderful, Bob," she said. "I was sure I'd have to go through this whole project without seeing the inside of Antoine's. I've been hearing about it since college."

"Their reputation is well-earned," said Dr. Jennings. "But you'll get to know their menu well enough. You live near Tulane, don't you?"

"I wonder what you *don't* know about me," said Dr. Short.

"We'll find out tonight. Do you like oysters Rockefeller?"

"We'll find out tonight."

"Fine," said Dr. Jennings. "I'll go home and call Paul, my regular waiter. Is seven-thirty all right with you? I'll come by your apartment around six-thirty, so we can take a leisurely ride downtown. They used to have a streetcar line on St. Charles Avenue here, up until a few years ago. It's a shame you never saw it. The trolleys were much more picturesque than San Francisco's, I think."

"I'll have time to put on something special, then," said Janet Short. "I'm looking forward to it, so don't be late."

"Not me," said Dr. Jennings. "I have the secrets of the universe on my shoulders. I *need* a rest."

CHAPTER 2

The next morning Janet Short arrived at the IAY Center half an hour before she was due, thinking that she could get a head start on the new material. She was chagrined to find that most of the other supervisory personnel were already hard at work. She picked up her lab coat from her locker and went straight to her desk, skipping her usual morning coffee. Benarcek was in the Data Retrieval Resource room, a cup of strong Louisiana coffee and chicory in one hand.

"Good morning, Justin," said Dr. Short. "Financing something with overtime?"

The young analyst turned away from the CRT that he had been studying. "Oh, good morning, Dr. Short," he said. "No, I'm just . . . well, kind of curious, I guess. This stuff here doesn't mean much to me; I was only sort of hoping it's the real thing, if you know what I mean."

Dr. Short knew exactly what he meant; she felt the same way. Perhaps by the end of that day they would know whether there might be other intelligent beings awaiting them in the universe. The young chief of the Data Retrieval Group understood that the final analyses might take months; even if Dr. Jennings's answers *were* buried among the baroque equations, many thousands of man-hours were required to dig them out. But, how much more engrossing the work would be, with such a definite goal in view!

"Okay, I was just kidding," said Janet Short, sitting down at her desk. "What are you looking at?"

"Haven't you seen this?" asked Benarcek. "This is the end of the red system's output. The last few transformations. I guess what we want is locked in these diffycues."

"Not necessarily. In fact, the real information is probably somewhere earlier in the last third of the output, not at the very end. So the red's stopped grinding it out?"

"It stopped about three this morning."

"Well, that's a good sign," said Dr. Short. "What do we do now?"

"I assume we proceed with the certification," said Benarcek.

"Of course," said Dr. Short. "I was just thinking about all the work we have to do and wondering where to start. We can't count on this data being legitimate. We'll have to study the documentation, going on the theory that there actually was a bug in the system. It's up to Dr. Jennings and the astrometrics sharpies to sift the numbers for meaning. I sure hope that it's all genuine, though. It would be an awful letdown to start over, now."

"That's for sure," said Benarcek, clicking off the CRT. "I have to run through the post-go checkout, I guess. Do you want a fiche of the system's afterbirth?"

Dr. Short grimaced at the jargon. "All right, Justin, but mark it plainly. This material was supposed to take months to accumulate. I'm being swamped by data, and I can see myself going loony in a couple of days."

"Right, Dr. S.," said Benarcek. "You know, if these relay buckets can spot spacemen for us, I think we ought to try to program them to grant wishes next."

"You're a skeptic," said Dr. Short. "Where did you go to school?"

"Yale," he said, holding up his right thumb and grinning.

"That figures. They should only hire guys from state schools here," she said mischievously. "They drink too much beer, but at least they're quiet to have around."

"You're a pretty typical Wellesley type yourself, Dr. Short," said Benarcek at the threshold of her office.

"Case-Western Reserve," she said. "Now get to work." She laughed softly to herself as he left; then, with a sigh, she picked up the phone and began her own work.

"DSL, Miss Briarly," said the librarian's voice.

"Good morning, Chris, this is Janet Short. How's the PTP material coming?"

"It's all done, I think," said Miss Briarly, the Data Source Library's staff supervisor. "We were here until seven-thirty last night sorting the bulk, and the night personnel had all the fiche made up during the late shift. At least, they were *supposed* to."

Dr. Short gritted her teeth and held back her comment. "Do you think you could check on that now?" she said finally.

"Sure, Dr. Short," said Miss Briarly. "I'll be back in a minute. I'll put you on hold, all right?"

"Wait a minute, if you're going into the library. You're going to have a fiche of the red system's output, DRed. I have the first part of it already. I won't get an official copy until later, the way the routing in this office works. But I wonder if you'd do me a favor and lend me the library's."

"I'd surely like to," said Miss Briarly doubtfully, "but I figure Dr. Corangeli wouldn't want that to leave the library. I wouldn't want to take a chance with it."

"Right," said Dr. Short angrily, "I understand. Listen, I may be away from my desk for a moment. Don't put me on hold; just give me a ring when you check on the fiche." Then, without any further word, she slammed the receiver into its cradle.

Around her in the mansion, Dr. Short knew that great ideas were taking shape, but she could witness none of it. Her job required her to proceed as though nothing of importance had occurred; in fact, she had to continue as though the whole output of the newly-developed 440/65s was purely a waste of paper. She felt frustrated, and the pigheadedness of the librarian just aggravated her more. All her lfe Janet Short had noticed that certain people jealously guarded whatever tiny scraps of authority they might have. Perhaps that authority was their only source of identity. In that case, Dr. Short pitied them; but she hated having to pity anyone. She regarded it as an imposition. Empathy was one thing, but pity was something else, something completely unattractive.

After lunch she received a call from Dr. Jennings. "Good afternoon, Dr. Short," he said.

28

"You don't have to be so formal," she said pleasantly. "Especially after yesterday evening."

"I'm glad you enjoyed it," he said seriously. "But I can't afford to confuse my private life with my work. So between nine and five you'll be 'Dr. Short,' and I'd appreciate it if you'd not refer to me as 'Bob' in front of our co-workers. This project has an unprecedented importance, and we're going to need a certain discipline."

"Fine, Dr. Jennings," she said. "I understand perfectly."

"Good. Now, what I wanted to talk to you about. I've been speaking with the math and tech boys, and we're all pretty much convinced that the red output is legitimate. I want to pull you off the certification job. I don't suppose you'll mind too much."

Dr. Short laughed. "You have a gift for understatement," she said.

"In an administrative position, that's a valuable trait," said Dr. Jennings. "It won't be too difficult to train your Data Retrieval people to classify our astrometric findings. You won't have to comprehend the figures you'll be working with. There's nothing technical about the job. You'll recall that this transposition of departments was supposed to occur sometime around the end of September, and gradually, to avoid confusion. Well, the confusion's going to have pretty free rein for a while."

"What about my staff?" asked Dr. Short.

"I think you can keep all of your people, though personally I'd like to have a couple of them upstairs. You have a talent for hiring good workers; your group has been by far the most efficient in the project."

"Thank you, Dr. Jennings. We've just tried to keep our heads above water. The way things turned out, it's a good thing we did."

Now Dr. Jennings laughed softly. "You don't know how much. Anyway, I'm going to detach three or four of my starwatchers and put them under your authority, to maintain liaison. I'll send their profiles later this afternoon. And I've put your name on the top of the routing list for the finished, DRed output. That ought to be getting to you pretty soon. I'm having a preliminary report dupli-

29

cated, explaining what our initial impressions of the results are."

"Can you give me an unofficial hint?" asked Dr. Short.

"On one condition."

"You're going to keep a breakthrough like this from me on one condition? What is it?"

Dr. Jennings hesitated. "Tomorrow morning," he said. "I thought it was about time you had breakfast at Brennan's."

"Surely," she said, startled, "but what about keeping the work and the play separate?"

"I forgot," he said brightly. "About our results, though, we think most of the phenomena we've noted in the last twenty years has originated in the same area of the galaxy, and a lot of the other phenomena seem to be of an identical sort, even though they are more widely scattered. We think there's a chance that there is an intelligent race out there, making a certain segment of stars its home, traveling among them, leaving powerful broadcast facilities at its various stopping points. It's going to be a pretty unpopular theory, I suppose, but we're not about to suggest it publicly until we have all the proof we can squeeze from the computers."

"And what would you do if I were to rush into print with the story?" asked Dr. Short with mock seriousness.

"I'd do what everyone else would do. I'd laugh at you."

"I'll talk to you later, Dr. Jennings. You're nice, but you're strange." Dr. Short was smiling when she hung up the phone. As an afterthought she picked up the receiver and dialed the DSL number. Miss Briarly answered.

"I've been trying to call you back, Dr. Short," she said, "but your number's been busy."

"I know, Chris. I'm sorry. I just wanted to tell you that you can forget all that fiche we were so worried about. I don't need it, after all. Thanks, anyway." As she replaced the receiver, Dr. Short imagined Miss Briarly's furious reaction.

About three o'clock a young man in a white lab coat came into the Data Retrieval Resource room. Dr. Short didn't recognize him, and guessed that he was one of the astrometricists whom Dr. Jennings had assigned to her group.

"Dr. Short?" he asked. "I'm Stavros Karounis. I'll be working with you during the next part of the project. Dr. Jennings sent me down with these." He handed a fiche and a thick stack of papers to her. The fiche, of course, was the final product of the red system. Some of the papers were the profiles of the technicians that were to join the group; the bulk of the material, however, was Dr. Short's first problem.

"Would you like to fill me in briefly on this?" she asked. There were seventy-two pages of equations and data, none of which was at all meaningful to her.

"Sure," said Karounis. "Dr. Jennings would like to have this data analyzed as soon as possible. All that stuff comes from the red system. We used a code to represent everything in the original programs that might possibly indicate signs of intelligent life in the galaxy. After the red system is finished, we took the DRed output and sifted it for those coded statements. On these pages you have the sequence of statements that the computers did not reject as unlikely. Basically, Dr. Jennings wants these values in Appendix Two substituted in each equation or inequality, and a careful documentation of the results made."

"That's not such a difficult job," said Dr. Short. "It's just tedious. And if it's only plugging in values, that could be done almost as quickly on paper as punching the cards for the computer."

"Except for the fact that there are about five dozen different values to be tried in each instance. The machine will crank them all out in the proper order, and it'll be much simpler to go through and discard the trivial solutions," said Karounis.

"Now I suppose I'll have to scrounge desk space for you," said Dr. Short, once more feeling that she would be stifled by the details of office logistics.

"If you'd rather not," said Karounis, seeing Dr. Short's distaste for administrative problems, "I'll take care of settling myself in, and making up a corner for the three of us."

"Where are your two friends now?"

"Dave Franklin and Mary van Raale are still upstairs with Dr. Jennings. We have quite a bit of work to do before you finish the substitution program. I don't think they'll be coming down until you're done."

"All right," said Dr. Short. "Tell Justin Benarcek to clear an area of the DRG room for you. And ask him to come in here, if he's finished his checkout of the 440s. If he hasn't, have him send in Miss Neumann."

"Sure thing," said Karounis. "I don't suppose we'll be doing too much together until about the middle of next week. Until then, I'll try to keep out of your way. Computers have never impressed me as being anything more than just expensive adding machines. Being this dependent on them sort of scares me; I feel like I'm out of my depth."

Dr. Short smiled. "We're all beginning to feel that," she said. "Even those of us who were raised on computers."

Benarcek came into her office about twenty minutes after Karounis left. "I've got him all tucked in," he said. Dr. Short nodded and indicated that the young analyst should have a seat.

"Have you finished the post-ops on the red system?" she asked.

"No, not quite," said Benarcek with a guilty grin. "But I passed it off to Jimmy. I've got seniority or something. It's not that important any more, is it? I mean, Dr. Jennings just about guaranteed the output's validity. And I figure you have more interesting things to do."

"I suppose so," said Dr. Short. "I'm going to have to check this enthusiasm of yours. I don't want one job after another left unfinished just because there's something more interesting coming up. But look here. We have a fairly simple programming chore. The only thing is that it's vital. It's *got* to be done right. Here are all the equations for Project PTP that the computers approve off. And here are about sixty possible values for each of the variables. Every one of them has to be fed into every one of the equations. That makes a large table of final possibilities."

"But it isn't any problem for a 440," said Benarcek.

"That's what I told Mr. Karounis. But I've been reading Dr. Jennings's memo on these questions. I can't stress how important they are. So we're going to do the job in sections. There are seventy-two pages of equations; I'm going to have you program one of the 1515s to run the first half of them. Have Miss Neumann program one of the other 1515s to do pages eighteen through fifty-four. Then have Jimmy run through pages thirty-six to the end. We'll check on the overlapping parts and that ought to give an indication of the correctness of the rest. Hopefully, they'll match up. Meanwhile, I'll run the whole unit on one of the 440s. So much for zero defects."

Benarcek was nodding happily. "This is what I was hoping for," he said. "We have flying saucers and bug-eyed monsters right here in these equations. We have robots and ray guns and anti-gravity devices and everything I used to love so much when I was a kid. I want to get all this paperwork finished. I want Dr. Jennings to pull down a big old map of the Milky Way and take a long pointer and say, 'Ladies and gentlemen—*there*.' Then we can build our own super-tranmitter and say hello."

Dr. Short stared in surprise. "You're a romantic!" she said. "How did you ever get in here? One more outburst like that and I'll call the security guard."

"I'll get the others right to work on this," said Benarcek with embarrassment, picking up the stack of DRed output.

"Better leave that there for me to work on," said Dr. Short. "Calm down, Justin. You'll all get your own copies. Don't worry, the universe has been around a long time. Your spacemen can wait another few hours."

By four o'clock Dr. Short had drawn up a preliminary program for the first ten pages of the data. Each equation had to be given a coded address, and each of the sixty variables had to be given an identity tag. Wanting to check her progress, Dr. Short left her desk to find an unused computer terminal in the Data Retrieval Resource room. Her co-workers had had the same thought; there were three teletype terminals, all occupied at the moment. Dr. Short cursed quietly, then returned to her office to do some more of the program. At four-thirty she tried again. Once more she had no luck. Benarcek sat at one of the teletypes, feeding his preliminary program into one of the 1515s; Rachel Neumann was using the second terminal; and, at the third, Dr. Short saw a strange man, who she supposed was Stavros Karounis's colleague, David Franklin. She decided that she would make a final try in fifteen minutes, just to have the assurance of seeing a portion of the material working before she quit for the weekend.

At four forty-five the terminals were still occupied. In frustration she went to Benarcek's side and waited until he looked up. "Is it quitting time, Dr. Short?"

"Not quite," she said. "But if you're at a stopping point, why don't you go?" I've been waiting for a terminal for an hour, now. I'm happy to see the three of you working so hard. I wonder if you'll be so diligent a month from now."

"The three of us?" asked Benarcek.

"Well, you and Rachel and, I guess, David Franklin.'

"That guy over there? I don't know who that is," said Benarcek. "Dave Franklin's black, anyway."

"Oh, for goodness' sake," said Dr. Short, walking quickly to the third terminal. "Excuse me," she said firmly, "I'm Dr. Short. I'm in charge of the equipment here. I don't want to sound petty, but the machine you're using is essential to our work. If you like, I can schedule you in for Monday morning."

"I'm sorry, ma'am. I don't work here or nothing," said the young man, looking up uncomfortably. "Chris said I could just wait in here for her. I was just playing blackjack."

"What?" asked Dr. Short, still not quite understanding.

"I'm waiting for Chris Briarly," said the young man. "She said I wouldn't be bothering anybody if I sat here. These computers have all sorts of games on them. Demonstration things, I guess. I've been playing blackjack with the computer."

Dr. Short was very angry, but she controlled her temper. She looked at the long trail of yellow paper piling up on the floor. The teletype had just chattered a message: *Your winnings are now—Minus 540—dollars.* "You're not doing very well, are you?" asked Dr. Short.

"No, I guess not," said the young man, "but I'm playing against a computer. It's not that easy, you know."

"It's not stacked, if that's what you mean," said Dr. Short. "The cards are chosen with random numbers." She stared at the terminal, thinking how much she would like to strangle Chris Briarly. She gave up the idea of getting any work done that afternoon. Her thoughts were interrupted by the noise of the teletype: *How much do you wish to wager?***

"Do you want to play one?" asked the young man.

"No, I ought to get back to my desk," said Dr. Short. She reached over the boy's shoulder and typed in *20*.

Then the computer took over. The teletype sat silently for a few seconds, finally typing:

Your hole card is	*Jack of Hearts*
You are showing	*Five of Hearts*
I am showing	*Jack of Diamonds*
*Do you wish another card?***	

Dr. Short typed *yes*. The computer considered her decision. Then:

You draw   Nine of Clubs. You busted. Your winnings are now—Minus 560—dollars.

Before she could apologize for her loss, the teletype asked how much she wanted to wager. She typed in 40.

"The gambler's fallacy," said the young man. Dr. Short sighed and ignored him.

Your hole card is	*Three of Spades*
You are showing	*Two of Clubs*
I am showing	*Queen of Clubs*
BLACKJACK	
My hole card is	*Ace of Diamonds. Your*

winnings are now—Minus 600—dollars.

*How much do you wish to wager?***

Janet Short hit the zero, and while the young man complained, the terminal spelled out all the post-go information. Dr. Short noticed the relatively large amount of computer time the boy had used. "I'm sorry," she said. "This is probably the worst possible place for you to hang around. From now on, if you want to wait for Miss Briarly, please stay in the front parlor. The security guard and the receptionist should never have allowed you in here." The boy looked exasperated and got up to leave. Dr. Short saw Chris Briarly coming to meet him; Dr. Short knew exactly what he would tell her, and what the librarian would think. She was too tired to care.

The next day was Saturday. Bob Jennings had made reservations, and she took the bus downtown to meet him at the corner of Canal Street and Royal. It was eleven-

35

thirty when she arrived in the Quarter, and their reservations at Brennan's were for noon.

"Isn't it a little late for breakfast?" she asked.

"Not at Brennan's," said Jennings. The day was clear and quite hot already. Jennings was a completely different person outside the project. Dr. Short was amazed at how easily he forgot his cares and duties. "I have to," he explained. "Making up answers and excuses to the bosses in Washington takes up most of my time. It is also, by unhappy coincidence, the single worst thing I've ever had to do. So if I left the office and went home to worry some more, I wouldn't last another month. Then you'd have to break in a new supervisor, and the world might never find out all the wonderful things I have planned for it."

Dr. Jennings was a strong man to have accepted the responsibilities he had been given. And Dr. Short knew that despite his frequent complaining outbursts he loved his job, and wouldn't ever think of delegating more of the work than was absolutely necessary. He was tall, not particularly well-muscled, but still athletic in a trim way. His brown hair hung over his forehead, and his beard was cut and trimmed carefully, giving him the look of a slightly bewildered professor of freshman English, rather than a brilliant astronomer and mathematician.

He held Dr. Short's arm casually, guiding her through the weekend shoppers that crowded Royal Street. At last they came to Brennan's, one of New Orleans's best-known restaurants. Like many of the famous dining spots in the French Quarter, the outside looked almost unpromising. The inside, however, was another thing entirely. The dining rooms were luxuriously and beautifully decorated, situated around a large, picturesque old New Orleans courtyard. They took seats by the fountain and enjoyed cocktails while they waited for their table. The meal itself was a lesson for Janet Short—Creole cream cheese Evangeline, eggs Sardou, about the best French bread she had ever eaten, strawberry crêpes Fitzgerald, and dark New Orleans coffee. She had thought for years that the best a restaurant might offer was just another big steak. "If you order a steak, ever, when you're with me," Jennings had said once, "I will personally drag you to the banks of the Mississippi and throw you in." He had looked serious.

Later, after they had eaten and stepped back out into the hot afternoon, Janet Short looked at her project director. "You shouldn't think that it's your duty to keep a poor Yankee girl entertained," she said.

"'Duty'?" asked Jennings, with eyebrows raised. "What do you mean? I think you've been spending too much time with your bytes and bits. We're courting, aren't we?"

"I hadn't noticed that," said Janet Short, frowning a little.

"It's still in the early stages; don't let it worry you. It'll all sneak up on you when you least expect it."

Dr. Short studied his face for a moment. "To tell the truth, that's something I hadn't expected at all. I've been too busy."

Jennings shook his head. "And I'm going to keep you busy, too. That's my best strategy, you know. Won't give you time to think. I figure Le Ruth's for dinner, then a river cruise, moonlight and waves, tonight about nine. And we finish off at the Cafè du Monde with coffee and hot *beignets.*"

"Well, you certainly have it all lined up. What about tomorrow?"

"Sunday?" asked Jennings. "Sunday I have to go through the summaries from my department heads, what they've accomplished this week. Then I have to try to make a master key. I connect as many of the variables with actual star locations as I can. I ought to wait until the whole substitution program is finished, but I'm going to give a try anyway, maybe get a head start on it."

"What kind of courtship is that?" asked Dr. Short. "Am I going to play second string to your work? Sit alone nights while you count white dots on photographic plates?"

"We use negatives and count black dots. It's easier. You could help me tomorrow, if you want."

"I'd rather play blackjack," she said. Jennings looked at her uncomprehendingly, and she just laughed. "Have you given any thought to what this project might do to the public? There's bound to be all kinds of political and public reactions. I mean, just the philosophical question alone. What do you think the Church will say? How will people feel, when we're no longer the lords of the universe?"

"Washington has another research group working on that right now. They're in Kansas City. It's not our concern."

"I don't see how you can say that," said Dr. Short, wondering just how serious he might be. "You sound like a crazy scientist from a horror movie. *Certainly* it's our concern."

"I was only kidding," said Jennings. "I don't want to think about it too closely, though. I've already lost a good deal of sleep over the idea. We'll learn how mature the human race is; I'm not exactly sure that I want to know."

"I know what you mean," she said. "I suppose there's a chance the project won't learn anything dangerous, though."

"We're almost certain that we've been receiving transmissions from a single source in space. Within the rest of the galaxy the locations of certain other radio sources follow too strict a pattern to be pure accident. That suggests intelligence. What else can you deduce from that? And what happens when we finish the substitution program, and our math experts intersect their lines and come up with Martian invaders or whatever?"

"Justin Benarcek can't wait for that," she said, trying to avoid facing the threat in the idea.

"And I can't wait, and you can't, either," said Dr. Jennings. He pointed to the many people sunning themselves in Jackson Square, listening to a jazz band playing beneath the swaying fronds of a banana plant. "But what about them? What are those poor people going to do?"

Janet Short couldn't answer. She just looked toward the French Market; after a moment's silence, she suggested they buy a couple of melons for later.

CHAPTER 3

The Victorian mansion on St. Charles Avenue that housed the New Orleans Center for Coordinated Astrometrics had once had a large, comfortable library. The thick wine-red carpeting was still there, and the huge, polished oak doors. The brass fixtures were showing their age, and in places the plaster on the walls showed ominous cracks, the first signs of eventual decay. The shelves which lined the walls had been emptied of their books; leatherbound sets of MacBurnie's essays, the complete poems of Catherine May Lidsake, the plays of August Anthony Bettle had been given to charity organizations. Their places had been taken by card catalogs and journals of scientific associations; one wall, previously given over to the original owner's collection of Louisiana literature, now stored boxes of microfiched reference works. More than a month after the red system's revelations, Dr. Robert L. Jennings, Jr., assembled his entire staff in this room. The library was very comfortable; it induced a mood of relaxation and a feeling of pleasant cooperation.

Dr. Jennings stood at a podium, facing his research team. Behind him were two charts and a blackboard. One chart and the blackboard were covered with figures and abstruse mathematical operations. The other chart showed the great spiral swirl of the Milky Way galaxy, with several red lines running through and intersecting at points marked with large circles.

Dr. Jennings had been talking for some time, describing

39

for his audience the assignments of each department; even the secretaries and office help were present. The whole story of Project PTP unfolded in simple terms. The more sophisticated scientists listened with interest to the findings of their colleagues and the data-collating committee. The untrained personnel were amazed by the planning involved in the great investigative venture; it seemed on the verge of solving the final problem.

"Mr. Crossier," said Dr. Jennings, "would you be so kind as to play that tape now, please?"

"Sure, Dr. Jennings," said the boy, a local high school student who had been employed by the project for the summer. He reached across a large tape player and pressed a button. The library was filled with a loud, persistent crackling. It was an irritating static with occasional, seemingly random, squeals and barks.

"Listen for a moment," said the project's director. "That's the sound of deep space, ladies and gentlemen. That's the material we've sifted so diligently these last few weeks. All the punched cards and spools of tape we've collected represent bits of that crackle or scraps of hum. This noise did not originate near the Earth. Indeed, little of it is from our solar system. Some of it has traveled the full length of the universe to reach our ears, from sources billions of miles away."

Even the most knowledgeable people in the room sat silently, staring at the tape player. The only sound was the eerie voice of the cosmos, never dying down completely, often punctuated by strange bursts of noise. One had to wonder what long-dead celestial events caused those sudden chatters of static. There was, of course, no way of knowing; the astronomical sciences as yet had only a collection of theories to explain what happened at the distant limits of the observable universe.

"Let's remove from this tape the noises we can readily understand and classify," said Dr. Jennings. He nodded to Crossier, and the boy stopped the machine; he ran the tape forward to a designated place. With the tape player silent, Dr. Jennings went to the chart of equations. "First, there's the background wheeze of the universe," he said. "In 1965, two scientists discovered that we receive a constant radio emission from all parts of space around us. This radio phenomenon corresponds to a temperature of three degrees Kelvin, the present temperature of interstellar space. Measurements of cyanogen absorption have enabled us to identify and tag this steady noise." Here he indicated a line of equations and a diagram of an oscillogram representing the three-degree Kelvin component. He nodded to Crossier, who started the tape machine again.

The noise filled the library once more, sounding to the audience the same as it had before. "We've eliminated that background crackle from the original recording," said Dr. Jennings. "Can anyone detect a difference?" A few people shook their heads. "I didn't think you would. In comparison to some of the other noise components, the background stuff is pretty inaudible. But it comes from everywhere, between the Earth and the moon, between our solar system and Alpha Centauri, between our provincial wing of the galaxy and the hub, between our island galaxy and the others. Everywhere throughout the vast vault of space, the failing glow of the incredible heat generated at the birth of the universe whispers to us." He indicated that the boy should once again skip ahead on the tape.

"Our sun gives off energy in the form of electromagnetic activity. Some of this we can detect easily, such as light in the visible spectrum. Other forms we need instruments to record. Now listen to the muttering of our own parent star." Crossier punched the button, and the audience heard a steady, low static. "Even the planets join in the chorus," said Dr. Jennings, "though their contributions are extremely minor. Now we'll hear the sound of the skies, with the static of the sun and planets plus that of the background radiation removed." Once more the tape played, and again no one could detect much lessening of the noise level.

"All right, so much for the pitiful squeaks of our neighborhood." Dr. Jennings pointed to several lines of figures enclosed in a black box on his chart. "These are pulsars," he said. "Since 1968, hundreds of astronomical objects have been identified as pulsars. A pulsar, as its name indicates, gives off a pulsating radio signal at regular intervals. We have learned in the last twenty years or so that the individual rate of each pulsar is slowing down.

41

For instance, the pulsar in the constellation Horologium was measured in 1977 to have a period of .154 seconds. It is now measured at .1565 seconds. We think pulsars are the final remains of old supernovas, star matter that has collapsed on itself and become incredibly dense. Our sun's diameter is eight hundred sixty thousand miles; pulsars may contain as much matter as our sun, but they are probably little more than about ten miles across. The pulses likely come from an area on or near the tiny star's surface. The short period between pulses indicates that the pulsars are rotating extremely fast.

"'Quasar' is a word coined to represent the phrase, 'quasi-stellar radio source'. Quasars are the source of both high-gain radio and visible radiations. Some quasars throw out the equivalent of all the radiation produced by our entire Milky Way galaxy; these are the *small* ones. A number of recorded quasars emit a million times that much, a million times the radio noise of one hundred billion stars.

"You'll agree, that's an awful lot of static. Whatever produces it must be very strange in nature, unlike anything familiar to classical astronomers. It was thought for years that these 'radio stars' were relatively small and relatively near. Now we know that they are quite the opposite; they are immensely huge and as far away as they could be. A quasar throws off the equivalent radiation of an object several light-years in diameter. It is only their fantastic distance that dulls the noise to the level we receive. Quasars are the most distant things in the universe, out on the very edge of the universe that man can explore with his instrument-aided senses.

"Now listen again to the tape. This time we have subtracted all that we've talked about, plus the noise of pulsars and quasars." He pointed to the black-outlined box of equations, while Crossier started the tape machine. This time there seemed to be a noticeable decrease in the static; evidently the audience was impressed by this form of deductive astronomy, for there was a brief moment of whispered comment.

"Our own galaxy," said Dr. Jennings, "the Milky Way, has a recognizable voice. Interstellar clouds of gas and dust emit large amounts of radio energy. For instance, the familiar Crab Nebula produces large amounts of static. Another source, in the constellation of Cassiopeia, is rated at about 10^{24} kilowatts. Now let's wipe the transmissions of our galactic nebulae off the tape." He waved to Crossier again, and the tape was once more a little quieter.

"Let's look at two more important sources of radio noise," said Dr. Jennings, pointing to the next cluster of equations. "Both of these sources are constant, and they're easily measured. The first is the radio emissions given off by one hydrogen atom in the depths of space when it collides with another in the proper fashion. Because of the near-perfect vacuum of the interstellar reaches, the laws of chance say this event will happen once in every eleven million years for each hydrogen atom. But space is infinite, and the hydrogen has been around for a long time. We have a regular background noise produced this way, at a regular and unvarying wave-length of twenty-one point one centimeters. At the opposite end of the scale, we have the biggest broadcasting station in the universe—a pair of immense spiral galaxies that are in the midst of a catastrophic collision. Out in the constellation of Cygnus we see the light that departed this unimaginable disaster over two hundred million years ago. The smashing of suns and the superheating of gases puts out 10^{33} kilowats. We'll hear what's left of our diminished noise after the hydrogen atom sigh and the intergalactic concussion are removed." The tape played, and the audience had to keep still to hear the residue of sound: an erratic crackle, an oscillating hum, and a few random squawks.

"Of course, there are sources of static besides the ones I've mentioned. Months of research produced these final equations, which list every source we know about, down to the very rushing of the planets and stars through the attenuated gaseous 'atmosphere' of outer space. Now we'll take out all the radio sources that man and computer can identify." Crossier started the recorder one last time. There was still a tiny, crisp, nearly inaudible static. Dr. Jennings walked to the tape machine and turned up the volume. The scientists and their staff sat in the room, looking at the tape player, struck silent with curiosity and wonder. At last Dr. Jennings snapped the machine off and walked back to his podium.

"That, ladies and gentlemen," he said, "is the upraised voices of our neighbors, shouting through the thin walls of our galactic tenement."

"How can you be sure?" asked Dr. Chareaux.

"We can't be absolutely certain, of course," said Dr. Jennings. "But, as I've shown, we've accounted for all the radio activity that we know exists. We allowed a large, generous margin for doubtful cases. We allowed for such things as the magnetic fields set up by the motions of the galaxies themselves. The computers worked with all the data we could cram into them, and decided that some of the radio sources were not natural. We have a collection of patterns and radio-wave signatures. That last stuff on the tape doesn't fit any of them. So we think we've found what we were looking for."

Justin Benarcek raised his hand, somewhat hesitantly. Dr. Jennings nodded. "What is it, Justin?"

"I was wondering if you could tell us where the broadcasting was coming from?" asked Benarcek.

"Of course, Justin," said Dr. Jennings. "I suppose that's the next most important thing. We had to find the noise, separate it from that huge overlay of other sounds, and trace it back to its origin, with the help of the two great radio-telescopes at Jodrell Bank and Arecibo, Puerto Rico." Dr. Jennings took his pointer to the other chart, the map of the Milky Way galaxy. "Here, ladies and gentlemen," he said, "here are our rivals for God's attention." He stabbed the pointer down on one of the intersections of red lines. Dr. Janet Short looked toward Benarcek, wondering if the young man recalled how he had wished that Dr. Jennings would do just this very thing. He sat in his seat tensely, leaning forward, his hands grasping the arms of the chair. Dr. Short smiled and returned her attention to her supervisor.

"This is a star called Wolf 359," he said. "Next to Alpha Centauri and Barnard's Star, it is one of the closest stellar bodies to our own solar system. Because we believe the radio transmissions are made by intelligent beings, and necessarily weaker than cosmic events, the proximity of the source is another factor that supports our theory. There may be many other artificial radio sources in the galaxy, but our receivers lack the sensitivity to record them."

Dr. Jennings moved back to his podium. He put down his pointer and folded his hands. "There, my friends, is our result. What we know about Wolf 359 has been typed up and duplicated; each of you is welcome to a copy, though the material is pretty technical. The star has little to recommend itself other than its relative nearness.

"To some of you, I guess, this doesn't mean anything more than the end-product of a lot of paperwork. It may seem that we've done only a summer's wild-goose chase, and it's time to move on to the next assignment. Maybe so. But if you feel that you weren't paid enough for your labors, try to console yourself with this thought: you'll always be a minor footnote in the annals of science. If we're right—and I, at least, am staking my future on it—then we've beaten out Armstrong's moonwalk and Tcheviol's Marswalk for historical significance.

"Okay, that's about it. Many of you are here for the last day. Thank you again for your work and your cooperation. I'll see the rest of you on Monday. We have to figure out what to do with all this."

The meeting broke up, and a crowd gathered around the podium, everyone wanting to question or congratulate Dr. Jennings. Some of the scientists formed their own excited groups, and some of the others just went home. Dr. Short watched the director from her seat. Although he had suggested that the project was almost completely finished, she knew that weeks of work remained. The tedious research had been concluded successfully, but the job that faced Dr. Robert L. Jennings, Jr. might prove even more difficult—the gentle handling of the bureaucratic authorities of the International Astrophysical Year.

Jennings looked very tired. It was plain to Janet Short that he wanted nothing more than to leave that hot library room; his colleagues, however, were far too aroused to let him off so easily. Dr. Short rose from her seat and went up to him. When she reached the small crowd around the podium she cut through as politely as she could.

"Dr. Jennings?" she said, trying to pry his attention from a furiously gesturing astronomer.

45

"Yes, what is it, Dr. Short?" he asked.

"I'm sorry to interrupt," she said with a worried expression, "but the operand addressor drums have to be re-allocated before I leave tonight, and you said that you wanted to speak to me about them."

"Certainly, Dr. Short," said Dr. Jennings. "You'll forgive me, people. Excuse me. I'll talk with you all on Monday." He took Dr. Short's elbow and together they made their way to the door.

Once out of the library chamber, he turned to her. "Janet," he said, "what the hell is an 'operand addressor drum'?"

"I just made that up," she said with a sudden smile. "I figured that you wanted to get away."

"You don't know how much," he said. "Thanks. I think my sanity was at stake."

"And mine will be, soon," she said. "If I don't get something to eat, I think I'll just fall tragically beside the 440s. You'd have a tough time explaining that to the Group Two people."

"I've got enough to explain to them," said Dr. Jennings. "Tell you what, Janet. Maybe we could get a quick snack now. Then we'll hop in the car and I'll treat you to the best duck dinner you've ever had, and the nicest ride, too."

"I don't know how you keep coming up with these places, Bob," she said, as they left the building. "I thought New York was the best place in the country for restaurants. But New Orleans is something special."

"Quiet, we don't want too many people to find out. We like it the way it is." They walked slowly down the gravel path to Dr. Jennings's car. The vehicle represented another facet of his personality, the rougher side that he tried so hard to keep hidden; it was a facet that intrigued Dr. Short very much. He drove a Messerschmitt E-5, a low-slung car that threatened speed even standing still. "Where would you like to go for something to tide you over until dinner?"

"That depends," she said. "How long before your duck dinner?"

"It's in Baton Rouge," said Jennings. "If we drive slowly, an hour or so."

"If we drive slowly. I can hold out that long."

Jennings smiled as he unlocked the doors. They drove up St. Charles Avenue until it ended at Carrollton; the steep green hill of the Mississippi River levee continued on ahead, with a narrow road paralleling it. Jennings cut across the main route and followed the levee. In a short time they had put the city behind and were driving through a strange countryside, by turns gorgeously rural and heavily industrialized. On one side of the River Road was the levee, too high to give a view of the wide, coffee-colored river. On the right side, however, were tiny towns of tarpaper shacks and dried-up gas stations. Between them were long stretches of woods of huge, sprawling oak trees hung dramatically with gray Spanish moss. Sometimes the trees would thin out and, suddenly, a ruined plantation house would glower in the setting sun. Just as Dr. Short's eyes would become soothed by the changing beauty of the scene, the greenery would end abruptly and instead there would be a monstrous, foul-smelling refinery of some oil or sugar company. Then a few hundred yards later would be another desperate town.

"Did you see that?" asked Janet Short suddenly, pointing to an immense tree standing alone in a field of waist-high sugar cane. It was bearded with Spanish moss and looked so perfectly like a symbol of the Louisiana region that she wished she had brought a camera.

"No," said Jennings, "but there are a lot of things to see along this road. On the way back tonight all these refineries will be lit up like Christmas trees, with bright lights along the catwalks and towers. They can be really beautiful."

"I've never seen anything like this."

"I've always said that an artist's heaven and a social worker's hell look a lot like Louisiana," said Dr. Jennings. For a time after that, they both rode on in silence, enjoying the rapidly changing scene beyond the car's windows.

After a while, Dr. Jennings turned to look briefly at Janet Short. "You know," he said, "all this time I've been thinking about the project."

He returned his attention to the road, and she wondered if he wanted to discuss something. "I'm not surprised," she said. "After all, you've been at work on it for months now. Just because the end is in sight doesn't mean you can put it all out of your mind."

"We're farther from the end than you realize," he said sourly. "Never mind the speech I made this afternoon. There is still too much work to be done. And, unfortunately, I have to do all of it."

"You mean the post-ops? That's what the whole Data. Retrieval Group is being paid for. You're not alone, you know."

"No, I don't mean the post-ops. That's just part of the cover-up, for the benefit of the foundations and Group Two. No, the real work is all mine. The real responsibility. I have to figure out what to do with what we've learned."

Dr. Short looked surprised. "You don't have much choice, do you? I mean, this is a public international venture. The IAY, remember? You just release the data to all the member nations, which means everyone."

"It's not that easy. I was given certain discretionary powers. If I want to, I can tie up all the findings as long as I like. The Project PTP employees signed security pledges when they accepted their jobs. Still, what I gave out today wouldn't do anyone any good. Just the name of a star. All of the real facts and figures are locked up in my office, in my keeping. I have a lot of authority on this thing, and it's starting to wear me down."

"I can't understand why you'd want to hide our work from the rest of the world, Bob," she said. "Besides making your reputation, maybe winning you a prize, you have a duty to perform."

"I have several, Janet," he said softly. "I'm beginning to learn that they conflict. So I give out all the pertinent facts, and the United States and the Soviet Union and China rev up their space programs and fifteen or twenty years from now we'll have three ships heading out of the solar system with squads of people dressed in khaki and brass. Then what will our friends from Wolf 359 think? My name will be mud in every cheap bar in the galaxy after that."

"It's not funny, Bob," she said. "Are you serious? Are you really worried about what's going to happen?"

"I'm serious. I'm worried. I don't care what happens to

48

me, personally. I was only kidding about that. But my name *could* go down in history alongside that of Attila the Hun if we don't handle it right. Never mind that, though; I'm really concerned with the reaction to the news, with the way people in general and the governments are going to respond."

"I don't know, Bob," she said. "I never thought of that. I suppose I'm still too idealistic. That's what hiding behind thinking machines can do to you."

"I've got an idea, Janet. I've been considering it for some time. Let me try it out on you."

"All right, Bob," she said sadly. "I don't know what good I'll be, but go ahead."

"Okay," he said, taking a deep breath. "Let me finish, please. It's going to sound bad at first, but let me get through the whole idea. I've decided that I'm not going to give IAY Group Two what we know. I'm going to release a statement that incomplete results were obtained, which our computers and the best minds assembled could not interpret entirely. Perhaps I'll admit that there are indications that another intelligent race inhabits the galaxy. That's exactly what everyone has been figuring for a long time, anyway. Then I'll write a detailed summary of our actual findings and give it secretly to the United States military."

"What?" cried Dr. Short, genuinely shocked. "That's awful, Bob. How could you seriously consider something like that?"

"All right, Janet, you promised that you'd hear me out. What's the best way of getting something like this lost in a tangle of red tape? You hand it directly into the bureaucratic machine. The Pentagon would be interested, of course, and maybe they'd even go so far as to appoint some sort of commission to make recommendations. Maybe they'd even invite me to advise them. But you and I both know that a project on the order of developing interstellar space travel is beyond the means of any single nation, even the United States. So eventually the thing would get filed away as impractical, nobody would ever find out, and Wolf 359 would be safe from our coffee grounds and eggshells forever."

"That's a pretty diabolical scheme, Bob," she said. "It's

kind of ugly." She was not at all mollified by his explanation.

"Forget it, Janet, I'm sorry I told you. It's my decision alone; I shouldn't involve you. So watch the road signs for me. I want to get on the main highway. It'll save a few minutes." They continued their ride, arriving in Baton Rouge some time before sunset. Didee's, their goal, was a pretty nondescript restaurant from the outside, but the house gumbo and the duck dinner with "dirty rice" were as perfect as Jennings had promised. Dr. Short couldn't enjoy the meal fully, however; her mind wouldn't stop thinking about Jennings's conflict and the way he had chosen to avoid it. She could understand the reasons, of course, but she didn't like them. She was silent during most of the ride back and even afterward, when they topped off the evening as usual with coffee and *beignets* at the Café du Monde.

The weekend passed pleasantly. On Saturday, Janet Short went across town to City Park, rented a skiff, and spent the afternoon sunning herself on the water. She spent Sunday with Jennings, poking into strange corners of the city. Ordinarily that would have been fun, but Jennings's presence reminded her of his dilemma, and she fell silent whenever he glanced at her. They ended the day at the Café du Monde, now nearly a ritual with them. She was glad when he left her off at her uptown apartment. She had done a great deal of worrying, and she was very tired.

CHAPTER 4

The next day she went to work on time. She had planned to arrive at least half an hour early, but at the last moment she changed her mind. The post-op schedule had been made up, and a copy was waiting on her desk. She looked at it distractedly, frowning while she sipped her morning coffee. Then she picked up the phone and called Miss Briarly in the library. "Good morning, Chris," she said. "I was wondering if Dr. Jennings had filed an official abstract of Project PTP's conclusions yet."

"No, I'm afraid not, Dr. Short," said the librarian. "It's sort of unusual, you know. He really should have written it up and filed it here and with Group Two before he made an informal announcement. I'm not criticizing him, you understand. It's just that there are routines and methods that ought to be followed."

"Sure, Chris. But the trouble is that I can't really proceed any further with the post-ops without an abstract. Do you have any idea where I could dig one up?"

The answer was obvious. "You could try Dr. Jennings," Miss Briarly said scornfully.

"I tried his office first. Miss Brant suggested that I ask you." Dr. Short knew that Miss Briarly couldn't be aware that the abstract was useless to the post-op chore.

"I'm sorry, Dr. Short," said the librarian curtly. "If I hear of this hypothetical paper, I'll surely tell you." She hung up quickly, and Dr. Short sighed. It seemed that Dr. Jennings was indeed going through with his plan.

Not more than an hour later she received a phone call

from him. "Hello, Dr. Short," he said. "I have to go up to LSU this afternoon with Chareaux and a couple of the others. I was wondering if you would accept the responsibility of locking up tonight. Miss Brant will give you a hand."

"Certainly, Dr. Jennings," she said, falling immediately into the staged formality they adopted during their working hours. She was pleased; here was an opportunity to put her own scheme into operation. After she finished talking to Dr. Jennings, she went looking for Justin Benarcek. She found him hard at work labeling and storing all the original blue-system material.

"Justin, could I talk with you a minute?" she asked.

Benarcek looked up from his work. "Sure, Dr. Short. There's a lot of stuff here, but it's not as complicated as it looks. What can I do for you?"

"I was wondering if you'd do me a big favor tomorrow. I have some work to do besides the post-op load, and the only time that I can find free is in the morning before nine o'clock. I'll need your help copying some documents. I may have some multilevel translation to do on the 1515, too."

Benarcek smiled and nodded. "Sure, Dr. Short. I owe you a half-day from last week, anyway." She thanked him and returned to her desk. About half past four she went up to Dr. Jennings's office. Miss Brant greeted her, and told her to have a seat while she finished filing some papers. After a few moments Miss Brant said that she'd get her raincoat and they could take care of locking up the administrative offices for the night.

While Miss Brant was gone, Dr. Short went straight to the files. From Dr. Jennings's conversations she had a pretty clear idea of where to search. It did not take her long; before Miss Brant returned, a thick file of Dr. Jennings's journal was in Dr. Short's folder, under her arm. The journal contained all of the director's notes, his ideas, and the complete set of computations and conclusions that he had used to make his announcement the previous Friday. But the journal now in Dr. Short's possession was in more rigorous scientific terms; it would be appreciated by even the most dubious of the world's scientists.

She made careful copies of the journal the next morning. Benarcek saw little of the actual material and didn't understand what he was helping Dr. Short to do. Later in the day, just as Miss Brant was leaving on her lunch break, and before the secretary's noon replacement arrived, Janet Short slipped the file back in its place.

Three days later a copy of the data was in the hands of every major authority in the field of astronomy among the member nations of the IAY. The furor over how the information became public did not abate for months. In that time, Dr. Jennings had to explain frequently, and his own reputation suffered more from the hint of his thwarted treachery than it gained from his part in the great discovery. Dr. Short watched helplessly as he was hounded and demeaned by newspapers and his fellow scientists. She felt terribly guilty; she could no longer stand to see him, though she was still certain that she had done the right thing.

And Dr. Jennings, who for so long had carefully guided her actions, knew that she had done the right thing also, although he could never tell her so. Thanks to his devious scheme, the Pentagon would never have sole possession of Project PTP. The US military had been more than just "interested" from the beginning of the project, and had often let Dr. Jennings know that they would consider prior notification of any positive results an "act of patriotism." The data now belonged to everyone, as he had always intended that it should. He was disgraced now; it seemed to the world that he had been about to sell the information to the United States government, and the honor of the project was saved only by Dr. Short's courageous act. That did not matter to Dr. Jennings. That was the way it *had* to be, the only way Jennings could balk the forces that watched him so greedily.

The inhabitants of Wolf 359, whatever they were like, were safe. For at least a little longer.

PART THREE

2021

CHAPTER 5

Dr. Justin Benarcek was asleep. According to the Lorenz-Corrected calendar aboard the deep-space vehicle, it was November 21, 2021. The ship had left the vicinity of Earth and its solar system nearly four years before. It was finally approaching its goal: Wolf 359, where radio transmissions had been detected by Project People To People over three decades earlier. Benarcek himself had received his first practical training in computer operations on that study. He was now fifty-seven years old, and one of the most respected men in the field of electronic data-handling applications. Computers had developed quickly in the latter part of the twentieth century; they had played a large part in the daily lives of almost everyone, whether the individuals affected knew it or not. By 2021 the eighteenth-generation machines, which were to those 440/65s as those computers were to a handful of fingers, were already being replaced by an even subtler nineteenth generation. The *Unexpected Guest* was equipped with several of the finest machines available at the time of the vehicle's construction, and they guarded the spacecraft's progress during the years while Dr. Benarcek slept.

It was dark within the spacecraft as it was beyond the vessel's plasteloid hull. No person could live under the pressures such as interstellar flight exerted; the solitary existence decayed one's sanity rapidly. The four years enforced a separation from every familiar landmark of a person's life. The mere distance from home, the impossible gulf of uncountable miles, wore down a person's spirit.

Through the tiny viewshields most of the stars were invisible because of the nearly speed-of-light velocity of the ship. Only those stars traveling at the proper angle to the line of flight could have been seen, and then, crazily, as thin, bright lines against the terrible flatness of space.

But there was no one conscious aboard to see them. As the *Guest* fell through that space, Dr. Justin Benarcek slept, his mind protected by the artificial pause created in his life. He dreamed, and around him the other members of the crew slept, also. The idea of maintaining all the travelers in full consciousness for the duration of the journey had never even been considered. Four years of supplies—food, clothing, personal effects, and, most importantly, entertainment—was a terrible burden, both to the design of the spacecraft itself and to the joint international effort that was paying for the voyage.

A person may dream many things in four years of sleep. A frequent, uneasy theme in Dr. Benarcek's dreams was the disgrace of Dr. Robert L. Jennings, Jr., the man who had done so much to guide Project People To People toward its goal. It was Dr. Jennings almost alone who discovered the signals from Wolf 359 and interpreted their significance. Under pressure from the United States government to suppress these findings for the sole profit of the U.S., Dr. Jennings had devised a scheme to free the knowledge for the benefit of the whole world. But his plan required that he himself appear to be a traitor, and for many years his name was hated and abused. Only after the passage of almost twenty years, with the publication of the memoirs of American officials and policy advisers who had been involved in the matter, and those of Jennings's unwitting accomplice, Dr. Janet Short O'Hare, was the entire tragedy understood. By then it was too late; Dr. Robert L. Jennings, Jr., had died in disgrace, six years before.

Dr. Benarcek had known Jennings well, had worked with him in a low-level technical position. When the story of Jennings's alleged betrayal had come to light, Benarcek had been appalled, along with the remainder of the scientific community. Jennings had been forced to resume his life under another name; Benarcek, after the initial shock, did not hesitate to denounce him as loudly as did everyone else. At the time, there could be no other interpretation for Jennings's actions: the man had sold not only the dreams of all mankind, but possibly those of the neighbor races of the galaxy, as well. The flood of posthumous honors and tributes to Jennings when the truth was revealed did little to assuage Benarcek's guilt. He never forgot how quickly he had begun hating. Often during the four-year sleep that thought returned to trouble him.

The computers monitored Dr. Benarcek's recurrent discomfort, and did nothing to alleviate it. Only if the dreams became extremely neurotic would action be taken. The shipboard computers also checked the crew's bodies. All somatic systems were monitored constantly; muscles were exercised on a cellular level by electric current; tissue and blood cell replacement rates were governed judiciously; even the growth of hair and nails was retarded.

Similar care had been taken to protect the crew's intellects. The minds of the sleeping people were allowed to function as normally as the situation would permit. Left with only pleasant dreams, a condition that easily might have been programmed, the dormant minds would have quickly stagnated and atrophied. A more imaginative and balanced approach had been taken.

This was the first manned interstellar flight, and it was a tribute to the cooperation of the world's peoples. It was also the expiation of guilt of scientists of all nations. The goal of the spacecraft was popularly known as Jennings's World; Commander Paul Drayden Leigh was due to be the first to set foot on that as-yet-unconfirmed planet, with a quotation from one of Jennings's speeches to read on that occasion.

Many things had happened in the world since that day in 1988 when Jennings's Infamy, as the newsfiche called it, was revealed. Nations had changed their borders, perhaps more often than in any time during the previous fifty years. The Soviet Union shrank in number of square miles but grew vastly in the ghostly realm of influence. China became a world power of a magnitude that dwarfed even the ancient glories of that land. Japan competed with the West in the economic arena and seemed on the verge of conquering its competitors; then the mighty empire toppled, the victim of blind growth and its perpetual dependence upon other nations for materials. England and France grew poorer; Germany united itself and struggled to take Japan's position as one of the leading manufacturing powers in the world. South and Central America starved and shouted, and frightened the world with the pure hatred of their revolutionary demands. The Middle East problems would not stay settled. Indonesia and the Philippines inherited the anguish that had almost destroyed southeast Asia. Africa demanded attention; the failure to develop the continent's resources and people disheartened its leaders. Africa, despite the forming of a continent-wide union of states, was still the most primitive area in the world, still a collection of factions with no other priorities than the gathering of food, land, and prestige.

Prestige. The word meant more in the world of the twenty-first century than ever before. That most ephemeral of international commodities had sapped the United States of most of its self-respect and leadership. Humiliated before the entire world in the Asian fiasco, then again in Guatemala and Honduras, and still again throughout the years with the inept, inhuman handling of its internal social problems, the United States sat stunned and almost helpless, unable to carry the responsibilities that had been so proudly assumed after the second World War.

More than ever before, the peoples of the world looked for guidance; they found it in a strange place. A new idea grew up to fill the need. One nation after another grew tired of the poverty and failure that were the common lot. The world's states began to understand that their plight was, after all, a common one. Nationalism became first an object of amused scorn, then horrified loathing. The Earth's people were united in misfortune. Not out of idealism, but rather out of a growing distaste for political maneuvering, they joined hands. There was no United Nations to govern; no, instead, the people themselves policed their own countries' representative officials. National boundaries still existed out of an administrative necessity, but a worldwide mood paid them little attention. Priorities had been simplified. National goals had been placed on a rational basis—providing the essential qualities of life, encouraging the development of every individual, ignoring national ambition as an outlet for collective energies. In such an atmosphere, Communism and democracy were beside the point.

The United States alone did not have the resources any longer to develop an interstellar craft. The Soviet Union and China were much too involved with the exploration of the planets and satellites in the solar system to be able to offer much assistance. If any attempt were to be made at direct contact with the inhabitants of Wolf 359, it would have to be a collaborative effort. And, somehow, that was how it seemed it ought to be.

This worldwide venture was reflected in the composition of the crew chosen to make the flight. The sleeping passengers of the *Unexpected Guest* numbered six, four men and two women. The commanding officer was Cdr. Leigh, a black man in his late forties, a citizen of Great Britain, and the first person other than a Russian to set foot on Mars. Perhaps no one else in the world had his experience in spaceflight; surely no one else could equal his skill and precision in the manual operation of spacecraft, a quality that would surely prove valuable in the latter stages of the journey.

Leigh had always been fascinated by the idea of space travel. He had been a young boy when Neil Armstrong landed on the moon; that was one of the clearest memories of Leigh's childhood. His family lived in Rhodesia at that time, and the lunar achievement attracted less attention there than in some of the more cosmopolitan areas of the world. Leigh had to be assured several times by his father that the event had actually happened, that it was not, as the boy wanted to believe, merely another science-fiction movie. Once convinced, however, Leigh hoped some day to follow Armstrong. Millions of other youngsters made the same wish. For Leigh, it was granted.

He not only walked on the gray dust of the moon's surface, but also through the dry red grit of Mars. Leigh was part of the personnel loaned by Great Britain to the United States in the first of the cooperative exploratory missions. He was one of the three survivors of that expedition. The others died tragically in one of the frequent, lethal Martian sandstorms. Leigh had carried the young female communications officer across three hundred miles to one of the Soviet camps. What happened on that trek was never detailed; the woman recovered from her injuries and, at the first opportunity, tried to murder Leigh. The third survivor, who accompanied them across the unmapped face of Mars, would not talk about it at all.

Cdr. Leigh slept, like Benarcek, under the protection of the spacecraft's computer battery. He would awaken first, when the *Guest* approached the vicinity of Wolf 359. His dreams, no doubt, were very different from Dr. Benarcek's, but the content of guilt and remorse, joy and pleasure was in the same, calculated proportions.

Next to him in the row of life-support niches slept Alexei Engerev, a Soviet astrophysicist from Byelorussia. Engerev served as an assistant to Benarcek and, as chief astrogator, was in charge of overseeing the operation of the computer plotting when they neared their goal. The electronic service units did most of the actual work; in fact, the original planning board argued for some time that Engerev's position was redundant. The answer was that on those grounds, *all* of the human passengers were redundant. The computers could carry out the entire mission more efficiently; but, as the idea was to send people to Wolf 359, they might as well have something to do along the way.

Engerev, like Leigh, had been on Mars, although several years later. Engerev was thirty years old. He was the only member of the crew to leave a family behind; he was considered a hero in the Soviet Union, and his wife and children were to be taken care of by the government.

His wife and children, unfortunately, were the prime reason he volunteered for the journey. Four years' travel time to Wolf 359, eighteen months maximum on the planet, and four years back to Earth—almost a decade. Engerev's wife, Ireyn, might well be dead, the children at least grown up and no longer his charges. It was an attractive possibility. He knew that it was the worst reason to sign on, from the point of view of the project; he was clever enough to hide his reasons from the psych board and qualified enough to please the selection board. As he fell through the limitless blackness of space, the face of his wife and the voices of his children filled his dreams.

The youngest member of the crew was huge Sanchito

Ajez, the Mexican medical officer. Ajez was only twenty-four years old. He had been only fourteen years old when the mission was first chartered. Until the *Guest* had raised ship from the isolated launching slip in western Australia, Ajez had never been off the Earth; indeed, until his journey to the Australian training compound, he had never left his native Mexico. He had been recommended for the position by his university professors. Only his remarkable record on the project's aptitude tests enable him to compete with the thousands of other applicants. Each member of the crew had been described in ideal terms by the project's electronic brains; the applicants were matched against these computer-drawn profiles; even the best credentials would do no good if discrepancies showed. Ajez matched the ideal medical officer's profile more closely than anyone else. The selection board was surprised, but Ajez was more surprised than they.

Of all the personnel, Ajez had the least experience, not only in the particular area of off-Earth exploration, but also in the more generalized field of his own choosing. He had received his M.D. at a much earlier age than usual, thanks to his exceptional talent and ambition. But he had as yet not gone out to practice medicine among his own poor people of the Yucatan peninsula. The selection board considered that his lack of practical experience would tend to make his crewmates lose confidence in him; the final decision was in his favor, however. If superior merit was valueless in the computers' decisions, then Ajez's shortcoming should be equally meaningless in the opposite situation.

Benarcek, Leigh, Engerev, Ajez. Those were the men who traveled the immense range of death among the stars, bound together in the armor of sleep. Along with them rode two women. Judy Swan Nkeida, from Niamey, the capital city of the All-African National Union, was the crew's linguist and social scientist. It was fervently hoped by everyone concerned that she would have something to study when the landing on Wolf 359 was achieved. The other woman was an American named Carolyn Giacomo. She was the project's military expert and was in charge of maintaining security. Her fellows prayed just as devoutly that she would *not* have anything to do on their new home.

Nkeida was a young woman, only a few months older than Ajez. Jennings's Infamy had occured almost nine years before her birth. She grew up in a poor section of Niamey; it could hardly be called a ghetto, because everyone in the city belonged to the same ethnic background, and Nkeida's neighborhood was set apart from the surrounding areas only by the poverty of its inhabitants. Niamey may have been the capital of the National Union, but it certainly wasn't a showplace, as many capital cities often are. Nkeida experienced years of desperation and frustration as a child, and it was only the strength of her personality and the sureness of her will that saved her from the life she had been born to.

Nkeida's parents named her Judy Swan, after a well-known black actress in America. That was about the last gift they ever gave her. Her father drank so much that he spent more nights sleeping in doorways than he did at home. Her mother tried to bring in whatever money she could, in whatever way she could. Nkeida grew older, and her contempt for her parents, for her people, and for the life they had accepted grew, too. She determined to escape; throughout her adolescent and young adulthood her life was guided by a desire to do what her parents did not, and to avoid what her parents had done before her eyes. She did not smoke or drink. She read omnivorously, because she had received the message that reading was a sign of mental superiority. Whether she had any special talents or not she didn't know; but the volume of reading that she did made it possible for her to see what her family and her neighbors could not: that there were boundaries to the neighborhood, and anyone could cross them if that person wanted to. Nkeida crossed them at the age of fifteen.

She had had little formal schooling, and she began the series of tests for the interstellar mission with a kind of lighthearted spirit of competition. She didn't expect to beat out all the other applicants; in fact, she wasn't precisely sure that she wanted to go, if she were chosen. But it presented an opportunity to learn just what and who she was, something that her parents and her environment had always kept cloaked in ignorance.

She slept as all the others slept, and she dreamed of failure. She dreamed that failure, the one thing in the world that she feared, would send her back to Niamey, to the alley where she had grown up, to the life she had rejected. She was of medium height, of regular, attractive features, of short, tightly curled black hair; she was a pleasant, charming woman, but she would never have confidence in herself. That was her heritage, and it disturbed her dreams whenever the shipboard computers said that it should.

Across the narrow aisle from her slept Carolyn Giacomo. She was quite a bit taller than Nkeida, and she was built solidly and strongly. Giacomo had been a track star for an amateur athletic association in Philadelphia, and had held the women's record for the 1500 meters for a short time. She was also an expert fencer and a master of *tai kwan do*, a Korean form of hand-to-hand combat. These things had occupied the greater part of her thirty-two years, and she worked hard to maintain her skills and her physical condition. She had tried to enter the United States Military Academy, but had been turned down because of her lack of scholastic aptitude. Still, she had served in the Marines, spending three years fighting the Guatemalan guerrillas.

She dreamed of many things. There wasn't a single unifying theme, as there was in the dreams of most of her fellows. If there was, it would have to be loneliness. But when that theme appeared, it made Carolyn Giacomo much happier in her sleep.

The idea of balancing the crew by sexes had been discussed for months. Arguments had grown heated; some experts said that there should be an equal number of men and women, others said there should be more men, a third group argued for more women. The possibility of petty jealousies among the crew members could spoil the entire mission. But it was finally decided that petty jealousies would occur despite what the selection board could do; if there were an equal number of men and women, there was no way of insuring that these people would pair off equitably, or that the pairs would remain happy for the entire eighteen months. "If these super-talented people can't live together for eighteen months," said one trustee at last, "then we might as well scrap the whole thing. We've spent a fortune drawing up psychological guidelines, and I think we'd better stick to them. They give us the best chance of coming up with mature and adjusted people. The hell with proportions." And that's what happened. The selection board picked the best candidate for each crew job and decided to let the men and women fight it out among themselves when they awoke near Wolf 359. After all, a year and a half isn't really that much time, and the crew would have an awful lot of work to do. That decision took a terrible load of pressure off the selection board; the board had been looking for ways to remove the pressure, and they were happy to find one. But more than one member still had private doubts. From then on, though, the doubts remained private.

According to the shipboard calendar, it was November 21, 2021, the day that human beings for the first time glimpsed at close hand a solar system other than their own. The process of awakening the dormant crew proceded quickly; Cdr. Leigh was brought to consciousness first, refreshed, in good spirits, feeling no hangover from his four-year slumber. He stood up and stretched, wondering at how good his muscles felt. He was in better condition than before the takeoff, thanks to the ministrations of the electronic monitoring devices. It did not occur to Cdr. Leigh to look out of one of the small ports; the one thing that he very definitely was not was romantic. It never occurred to him that he might still be on Earth, or in orbit around Earth, or in the middle of some uncharted part of the galaxy, near nothing familiar at all. These worries were the province of the astrogator, the Russian. Leigh had no curiosity.

He had his duties, though. These had been carefully prescribed for him in his training. He went about them now; in case he forgot or had some difficulty, he had a booklet to guide him. His first job was to check the others. One or more of the passengers might have died during the four years, or been rendered unable to continue. If the latter were the case, Leigh had the responsibility of terminating the life of a severely damaged crew member. Leigh sighed; it was an unpleasant way to begin a mission. But he moved slowly along the rows of protective arbors and checked the data provided by the monitoring equipment. Everyone seemed as healthy as he was.

The next thing Leigh did was to start the wake-up process for the others. This would have been done sooner or later automatically, but Leigh wanted it sooner. It was spooky, being alone in the dimly lit, humming spacecraft. The others would join him within an hour. Then he wouldn't have to do all the work by himself.

After that, Leigh lay back down and rested. Everything was in order. The only thing he could do now was get in the way of the computers. That was something he had learned from experience that he should never do.

A while later Leigh heard the sound of someone walking through the ship. He sighed; the mission had begun for him, and he would have liked to have a little longer to doze in his bunk. But now he had to get to work. He stood up and looked out into the passageway. "Engerev?" he called. "Who is it? Is that you, Engerev?"

The Russian astrogator peered around a corner. "Hello, Commander," he said. "I just woke up, and I thought that I'd better get things settled here."

"There isn't any hurry," said Leigh.

"We might not be where we want to be," said Engerev.

"In that case, there isn't anything we could do about it. What's the problem?"

"I think it would be better to know," said Engerev. "I'm switching the plotting from computer internal to external readout. I have a couple of hours of work to do. As I recall, you're supposed to see about the defrosting of the rest of the crew."

"I've already done that," said Leigh with some irritation.

"That job isn't finished until everyone is awake again."

"If something goes wrong, they'll tell me. I don't have to look for trouble."

"You expect Benarcek or somebody to come up and tell you that his arm is still frozen? Is that how you crossed the Martian desert? Not looking for trouble?"

Leigh was ready to turn his back on Engerev for the rest of the mission. "You don't have to look for trouble on Mars," he said. "And I expect I won't have to look far here, either." Then Leigh did turn his back, and walked away. He didn't like the Russian at all.

Within the hour, Engerev and Leigh were joined by Dr. Benarcek, Dr. Ajez, Dr. Nkeida, and Captain Giacomo. The crew went through a short period of welcoming each other, but the social pleasures were few and brief. Major Engerev went back to his work, Dr. Benarcek checked out the data processing equipment, Dr. Ajez checked his medical supplies, and Cdr. Leigh pretended that he had equally pressing work to do. Dr. Nkeida and Capt. Giacomo had little to do until they actually landed on the planet, and they passed the time trying to avoid cluttering up the narrow gangways in the ship.

"Well," said Giacomo, "here we are."

"Uh-huh," said Nkeida doubtfully. "Where is that, and what are we going to do about it?"

"Look out here," said Giacomo. "There's all kinds of stars. I wonder which one is Wolf 359."

"Probably that big bright one."

"Probably," said Giacomo, not noticing the edge of sarcasm in Nkeida's voice.

"I think I'll go back to sleep," said Nkeida.

"You can't," said Giacomo. "Not until it's time to go home."

"No," said Nkeida, yawning. "Not that. I mean sleep."

"Why don't you try to stay up a while longer? If you go to sleep, I'll be all by myself here then."

"You must have been a lot of fun in the jungle," said Nkeida. "I'll bet you even talked in your sleep."

"Some people did," said Giacomo seriously. "The ones who did ended up dead awful fast."

"That's certainly understandable," said Nkeida. "I bet they don't like bedwetters in the Marines, either." She didn't say another word, but went back to her bunk and took a nap. Giacomo stared out of the port; she felt as though she ought to be lonely, but she wasn't. She always wished that she knew how.

Justin Benarcek stopped by Engerev's cubicle "How's it going?" he asked.

"Fine, Justin," said the Russian. "I'm taking a spectogram now. I'll have it analyzed in about fifteen minutes. Then I compare it with the spectogram from Wolf 359, and we'll know if we're on the right block."

Benarcek nodded and left the astrogator to his work. Engerev seemed to be the only one who was taking the situation seriously. Leigh and Ajez seemed to be behaving as though they were on a bus trip to New Jersey. Nkeida and Giacomo acted as if they hadn't set out at all yet. Perhaps it would take a few hours before they realized where they were and what they had to do; after all, there had been no sense of traveling. Subjectively, it was only a few minutes since they had walked from the briefing room to the shuttle craft. They had been placed in suspended animation, and the four years had passed without their awareness. They were victims of the grossest jet lag in history. Their time sense was four years off.

Some time later, Engerev searched out Benarcek, carrying two sheets of graph paper in his hands. "Look," said Engerev, "we're all right. That's our star out there."

"That's a comfort," said Benarcek.

"What does that mean?" asked Engerev, annoyed.

"No, no. I'm not trying to sound like everybody else. I'm really glad that we're where we're supposed to be. I wouldn't have known what to do next otherwise."

"Okay," said the Russian, still mistrustfully. "But now that we're in the area of Wolf 359, we still have to find a planet. Something to stick a label of Jennings's World on. There isn't any conclusive evidence that there are any planetary bodies around this star."

"I suppose that's your job, next."

"Everybody's waiting on me," said Engerev. He paused, and Benarcek realized he was delaying the Russian astrogator. He muttered an apology and left. They had been awake so short a time, and already boredom and personality conflicts were beginning to cause discontent among the crew. It was small consolation to think that there was only another year and a half to go.

Dr. Ajez came by and asked Benarcek if he were feeling well. Benarcek nodded, but said nothing. "Depressed?" asked Ajez. "That's only natural, after awakening and realizing you've lost four years. And you're homesick, too, on a huge scale. And you have doubts about the success or failure of the mission, and the responsibilities are too heavy. Let me give you a mood elevator. I'm not going to be passing out pills for the next eighteen months, but today is a special circumstance."

"No, thank you," said Benarcek. "I think I ought to face all of this with my own head. The computer profiles thought that I could, and I'd hate to disappoint them."

"Don't think of the drugs as crutches," said Ajez. "I'm not going to let anyone abuse them. But situations like this are why they were invented in the first place. They have a positive place in my black bag, just as useful as sulfa and tongue depressors."

"Sure," said Benarcek. "See that Engerev doesn't fly away. And Leigh could use something, I guess. And Nkeida and Giacomo might just as well be popped out again for a while."

"But you're okay?"

"Not exactly, but I think I'll tough it out for a bit. Leigh is technically in charge, but I'm *actually* in charge. And I think it would help morale if I held a firm grip on the tiller and stuff like that."

"Whatever you say," said the young doctor. He shrugged and turned, going about his rounds. As soon as he left, Benarcek wondered if perhaps some drug might have helped him to function better. He was having one of the best fits of depression he had ever experienced. He just shook his head and tried to relax. There was nothing for him to do until Engerev found the planet.

Benarcek closed his eyes, thinking about all that had happened since the discovery that had made this trip possible. He had almost married one of the PTP job control people, a young woman named Amie. Benarcek laughed to himself when he thought how different his life might have been if he had done that. There was no way of telling what he might have done, how his career would have been different. He thought about Amie every once in a while, even though he hadn't heard from her in twenty-five years. He wondered what she had done, where she was now. He wondered if she remembered who he was, and if she was at all interested in what he was doing.

70

His thought went on in this vein for a while. The gentle sounds of the spacecraft lulled him, and the only interruption was when Alexei Engerev hurried into Benarcek's cubicle to announce that he had definitely concluded that there were at least three planetary bodies circling Wolf 359. This was the news Benarcek had been waiting for and dreading; if the report from the astrogator had been negative, the course of action would have been simple. They would have plugged themselves back in and gone home. Everyone on the mission and back on Earth would have been disappointed, but there would have been no other course of action open. The question of the radio noises would have gone unanswered, written off as a yet-not-understood freak of nature.

But there were planets.

"There is a planet about twenty-nine million miles from Wolf," said Engerev, consulting his notes. "There is another about eighty-seven million miles away from the sun. There's a third about one hundred nineteen miles. I have a possibility of a fourth about one hundred sixty-six miles, but according to the computer that one would be very unlikely to be hospitable to any kind of intelligent life. The same goes for the first planet, which would be a lot like Mercury. The second and third would be comparable, under the circumstances, to Earth and Mars."

"Can we get to either quickly?" asked Benarcek.

"Well, 'Mars' is on the far side of the sun right now," said Engerev. "It would take a few days to cross the system and meet it. But 'Earth' is almost directly in our path. I've already assigned the computers to plot an interception."

"Fine," said Benarcek. "This is all happening quicker and easier than I thought. Give your information to Cdr. Leigh and tell him that I'd like to speak with him whenever it's convenient." Engerev nodded and left. Benarcek went back to his daydreaming, although the subject had changed from his old love to the prospect of exploring a brand-new world. That was something he had given little serious thought to in the past.

Fifteen minutes later, Cdr. Leigh made an announcement over the ship's public address system. "Uh, ladies and gentlemen," he said nervously, "Major Engerev has informed me that we are in fact in the area of Wolf 359, and that there seem to be two planets belonging to the star which offer hope of finding native inhabitants. We are currently proceeding toward the most likely of these worlds, and we should arrive and begin orbiting sometime tomorrow afternoon. I guess we should all review the procedures involved, concerning the examination of the planet from orbit and after landfall. I would ask that you all review the safety precautions as written by the project's governing board. Once we land on the planet, our security will be the responsibility of Captain Giacomo, but I'm sure you all understand that in a situation like this one person cannot provide for all circumstances. To a certain extent we will be all on our own, and it would be best now if we all ran through in our minds just what our duties will be. It may be too late once we land." The commander's microphone clicked off with a grating noise, and once more the only sounds were the mechanical whines and hums of the ship. Benarcek wondered exactly what Leigh had said. He knew precisely what he was going to do after they landed on Jennings's World: he was going to follow everyone else around, waiting for Dr. Nkeida to make some decisions.

The day and the night passed quietly and without major event. When they awoke the following morning, a good deal of the space beyond the small port windows was filled with the giant green globe of Jennings's World. They approached the planet slowly, imperceptibly. They had not yet achieved orbit; that maneuver would occur around lunchtime, and it would be carried out completely by computer. Engerev had nothing more to do until he initiated the routines for the separation of the landing shuttle and their departure from the *Unexpected Guest*.

They remained in orbit around Jennings's World for three days. A good deal of film was exposed covering the planet in detail; the pictures were stored in the memory banks of the ship, along with elaborate analyses by Engerev, Leigh, and Nkeida. The orbit was changed every eight hours, so that they spent a while in polar orbit, another part of a day in an equatorial orbit, and in other paths designed to give a complete overview of the planet in the shortest possible time. Captain Giacomo

72

was the first to remark on the absence of lights in the night areas of the world; this was disturbing, as it indicated the lack of large population centers and, probably, the lack of scientific sophistication. Major Engerev pointed out that this kind of reasoning might be a bias they had brought with them, that a race without cities could not have technological progress. Dr. Nkeida agreed. Nevertheless, Dr. Benarcek stared down at the black face of the planet beyond the daytime terminator and wondered how people who could not even light their homes at night could send messages across the interstellar spaces. It did not seem likely. Despite Engerev's arguments about its being possible, it still didn't seem likely.

On the third day in orbit, the computer indicated that a radio source had been located on the apparently uninhabited land below. Engerev, Leigh, Benarcek, and Nkeida were excited by the news. After another orbit, the position of the radio source was confined and located. Engerev found the position on a map drawn by the computer based on the photographs that had been shot in the first two days. "Here," said the Russian. "It looks to me like some kind of beacon, a distress signal or something of that sort."

"In that case," said Nkeida thoughtfully, "it might not even originate here. The planet might be barren. The radio source we heard on Earth, that Dr. Jennings discovered, might have been planted down there centuries ago and forgotten."

"It might even be some kind of interstellar traffic signal," said Engerev.

"The main thing is that it demonstrates that *somebody* put it there," said Judy Swan Nkeida. "Whether we find him—or her, or it—is beside the point. We've proven the existence of life, somewhere in the galaxy."

"Would it be unscientific to celebrate?" asked Dr. Benarcek.

Major Engerev grinned. "When has that ever stopped anybody?" he asked.

And celebrate they did, although the party was a bit restrained. There were still tensions among the group members, things which the project's governing board had foreseen but had assumed the crew would be able to work out among themselves. They had chosen people with high degrees of intelligence and skill in their individual fields; along with that, the board hoped they had maturity and a reasonable approach to emotional situations. This hope may well have been naïve.

Cdr. Leigh was nominally in command, but both Engerev and Benarcek seemed to give the most orders. Giacomo and Nkeida, as the only two women, had a kind of competition, one that was pointless and cruel. Ajez often found himself reacting bitterly to the innocent remarks of his associates, out of a sense of inferiority which had been impressed upon him since the time of his selection. And the confinement and the perilous circumstances made everyone a little edgy, too.

The celebration was scheduled from 2000 hours until 2330, when the computers were programmed to begin the checklist for the countdown; the six crew members had to be aboard the shuttle boat, ready to land on Jennings's World, by 2359 hours. After the party, they had almost half an hour to get their equipment and research materials together.

A loud claxon went off at 2330, marking the end of the celebration. Wordlessly, all six people turned and went to their bunks and their storage hatches to prepare for the landing. There was no idling and no pleasant conversation. The preparations went on almost mechanically; no one asked if he might help someone else, no one asked for help in carrying the survival gear and the experimental packages to the landing craft. The six crew members were still desperately trying to assert their own personalities, and the main thing for them was avoiding any signs of weakness. It was apparent that each person had at least one unfriendly companion, who would seize that potential weakness and exploit it. It never occurred to the crew members that there was little anyone could accomplish exploiting another's weakness, not on this particular mission. Nevertheless, the struggle for prestige and power was a motivating factor among them. The Earthly computers had planned this, and had expected the six to carry the same attitude over into their individual work areas; the competition would encourage extra effort on each one's part in the exploration of the new planet.

The shuttle craft was loaded, and the six crew members strapped themselves into their padded seats. Cdr. Leigh went through the preflight checkout with Major Engerev. All the systems aboard the *Unexpected Guest* were shut down or reduced to minimum maintenance for the eighteen months during which the human cargo would be living on the surface of Jennings's World. A control panel inside the shuttle craft enabled Leigh to control the larger ship's computers and, through them, to make sure the *Guest* would be safe and ready for their return. When Leigh and Engerev were satisfied that everything had been done in accordance with the operating procedures as dictated by the project's governing board, they checked that the other four people were safely in their places.

"All set?" asked Leigh.

"Ready," said Benarcek. The data-handling expert was fighting off a nervous attack; he felt nauseated and hot. He wished that he could get up and walk around, or take a tranquilizer, but his pills had already been stowed away with the rest of his gear.

"So let's do it already," said Captain Giacomo impatiently.

"Americans," said Engerev softly, sarcastically. He reached above his head and flicked off a row of switches. There were several quiet hissing noises, and the shuttle craft moved slightly. Three long steel beams began to extrude from the side of the *Unexpected Guest*, a large hatch opened, and the shuttle rode out on the beams, away from the side of the spacecraft. Jennings's World appeared on the starboard side; all six people stared at the planet in awe. It was beautiful, different from any world in their home system. Where Earth was blue, and Mars red, Jennings's World was a deep, emerald green. The oceans were a lighter green, making swirling patches on the darker expanse of the land masses.

"I've programmed the shuttle to touch down in the middle of that central continent," said Cdr. Leigh. "Dr. Nkeida agreed that it provided the widest range of climate and terrain. If the continent looks like a failure, we can always move to another."

"We'll land in about ninety minutes," said Engerev,

checking his meters and dials. "Relax, everybody. Pretend you're on your way into Boston–New York Airfield."

The shuttle lifted gently from the three supporting beams and moved slowly away from the mother ship. There was little noise, as the larger engines would not fire until the proximity gauges indicated that it was safe. After a few minutes, the *Unexpected Guest* receded against the black velvet background of space, and Leigh manually threw in the two heavy rocket engines. Their path was in a braking orbit, spiraling down across the face of Jennings's World. After a while, the computers would use the thrust of the engines to slow them down even further, against the pull of the planet's gravity. Falling tail-down toward the surface, the shuttle would be slowed to a point where parachutes could safely be deployed. From then on, there was nothing to do until they landed. For Ajez, Benarcek, Giacomo, and Nkeida, there was nothing to do at all; those four tried to quiet their nerves and concentrate on their own jobs, but each found it impossible, each for different reasons. The trip from the *Guest* to the face of Jennings's World was the most harrowing experience in the lives of five of the six crew members, a fact that the project's computers had neither predicted nor prepared for.

Jennings's World came closer; the shuttle passed into the daylight sector, and the light from Wolf 359 drove the hard, cold stares from the sky. The green of the land below began to differentiate into forest and field, ocean and lake and river. The tops of trees of gigantic wooded hills waved and looked like ripples across the surging surface of the inland seas. Benarcek watched in silence, thinking about Dr. Jennings and the disgrace that man had accepted so willingly, just to promote the chance of this very mission. Benarcek thought about Dr. Short, who had married a chemist named O'Hare only a few months after Jennings's Infamy; Janet Short had gone into a life of almost complete seclusion, avoiding all interviewers and curious biographers. She never answered questions about her relationship with Dr. Jennings, especially after Jennings's death, even as the mission to Jennings's World became an actuality. She expressed no public interest, and turned down the opportunity to visit with the mission's crew and watch the takeoff. Benarcek wished that she could have been persuaded to see them; but her feelings were evidently strong and, of course, they were respected. He would have liked to say hello to her again, but he would never understand what she felt. Surely her memories and her mixed emotions were stronger than Benarcek's, and that must be a heavy burden, indeed.

Cdr. Leigh sat back in his padded seat and watched the planet grow to fill the forward viewscreen. The entire operation was controlled by computer; neither he nor Engerev had to do anything more. This was insurance against the possibility of injury or other incapacity to any member of the crew. The sophisticated computers on board could be programmed simply; everyone in the ship's company had been instructed in the procedures. If necessary, Ajez or Nkeida or Giacomo could raise the shuttle back to the *Unexpected Guest* and instruct the mother ship to return to Earth. In less than an hour and a half from the time of separation, the shuttle settled somewhat roughly onto the high, waving grasses of the central prairie of the main continent.

"We're here," said Leigh.

"Terrific," muttered Giacomo, unbuckling her belt and getting ready to disembark.

"You want to name the continent?" asked Engerev, looking toward Leigh, who was preparing his short speech.

"Huh?" said Leigh. He hadn't given that any thought.

"How about O'Hare?" said Benarcek.

"It sounds like an airport in Chicago," said Nkeida. "Besides, that would honor her husband, not her."

"You want to name a continent Short?" asked Ajez.

"Why don't we call it One?" said Engerev. "At least for a while."

"Fine," said Giacomo. "Sure. Let's get going. It's late afternoon out there. We have to scout around and set up a camp."

"We could stay in the shuttle," said Nkeida.

"You can stay in the shuttle," said Giacomo. "I didn't spend four years frozen solid and the better part of a week going in circles around this place just to sleep in the back seat."

"Check the atmosphere," said Leigh.

"Already have," said Ajez. "The computers can't find anything harmful in the chemical composition or anything odd about the organisms in it."

"Okay," said Leigh. "This is it, then. Is it cold out there or what?"

"Late spring weather, temperate zone," said Ajez. "Take along your raincoat."

Leigh inhaled a deep breath, pushed three buttons and, pulled a red knife switch. The hatch opened in the side of the shuttle; the air from outside rushed in, bringing strange, new odors with it. Leigh bent in the low opening and jumped to the ground. He paused down there to read his historic quotation, but everyone else was busily getting the equipment together, so no one heard Leigh. It didn't seem important; it wasn't.

After Leigh had climbed down to the grassy ground, Capt. Carolyn Giacomo followed, carrying a rifle across her back and a large knife in a sheath on her belt. In one hand she carried a pistol that fired explosive shells. "I'm going to be in charge for a while," she said. "Until we get a camp set up, and defended, we'll all be pretty vulnerable. We don't have any idea what might be out here."

"So defend us," said Leigh wearily.

Giacomo gave him an ugly look. "Commander Leigh, why don't you see if you can find some running water? That would be a relief on our bottled supply. If you can find a stream, don't drink any until Dr. Ajez has tested it out."

"You don't have to talk to me like that," said Leigh irritably.

"Oh, I'm sorry, I forgot," said Giacomo. "You're the hero of the Mars mission, aren't you?"

Leigh just stared at her, a light beading of perspiration making his black skin gleam in the strange light of Wolf 359. He did not bother to reply. He turned and started walking across the plain.

"Commander," called Giacomo, "don't you think you ought to take a weapon? You might run into a Russian or something."

Leigh turned around and took a deep breath. "There might even be a woman," he said. "But I doubt that. They're getting rare these days." He turned again and continued across the flat overgrown prairie. Behind him Giacomo laughed loudly and shrilly.

"What Russian?" said Engerev.

"Nothing," said Giacomo. "I wasn't talking about you."

"What do we do now?" asked the astrogator.

"We set up camp," said the woman. She pointed in the opposite direction from Leigh's path. "See those low cliffs? It might be safer there than out in the open."

"Safe from what?" asked Engerev. He received no answer, just a satisfied grin from Giacomo.

"Everything going all right?" asked Benarcek.

"Sure," said Engerev, spitting disgustedly, "just about the way I thought it would."

"We're going to set up camp in those rocks tonight," said Giacomo. "Here, take this pistol and check them out." She handed the weapon to Benarcek, who shrank back a step. Giacomo just held the pistol out steadily, frowning. Benarcek took it gingerly and started toward the tumbled mass of boulders. "There goes a good sport," said Giacomo.

"Oh, hell," said Engerev, "here we are on a brand-new planet. You don't send good sports out to look for campsites."

"Who would you send?"

"You."

"I'm busy," said Giacomo. "I'm guarding Commander Leigh's rear."

"Yeah," said Engerev, "guard your own rear." He turned and followed Benarcek.

Ajez and Nkeida came out of the shuttle, each carrying a backpack with their supplies and equipment. "That's it," said Ajez.

"Great," said Giacomo. She went to a small rectangular panel in the shuttle's side; there were five numbered dials. She set the lock in the correct combination, and the hatch closed slowly. Like the ship in orbit above their heads, the shuttle was now dormant, waiting for someone to set the dials in the proper unlocking combination. "Let's go," said the weapons chief.

"Where?" said Nkeida.

"I don't know," said Giacomo. "But you won't gather much information right here. Let's follow those two." She started after Engerev and Benarcek, who were already examining the rocky island in the grass. The dense growth reached up almost to Giacomo's face, and the slightly prickly stems irritated the skin of the six crew members. Nkeida started sneezing immediately; by the time they reached Benarcek, her eyes were red and swollen and her tongue and throat were sore.

"Do you want an allergy shot?" asked Ajez. Nkeida nodded. The Mexican doctor opened his bag and took out a pneumatic syringe and loaded it with an allergy suppressant cartridge.

"Our first crisis," said Giacomo cynically.

"This looks all right to me," said Benarcek, indicating a large cave.

"That's why *I'm* in charge," said Giacomo. "That looks like just the kind of place something will come home to and not like to find us in. We'll sleep out under the stars tonight. Under that overhang, though. Nothing will drop down on us, or sneak up on us from behind. We'll build a fire in front, and we'll be all right."

"Unless the moths on this world are attracted by fires, and grow to be ten feet tall, and suck blood," said Engerev.

"You stay up and watch for them," said Giacomo. "I'm going to eat and go to sleep."

Night was falling, slowly, as Wolf 359 dropped toward the horizon. The clouds turned a strange magenta color in the sunset; the sky overhead changed to purple, then a dark indigo, then black dusted with the ice white of stars. Still Cdr. Leigh had not returned. Benarcek suggested that someone be sent to look for him. Giacomo said that if something had gotten Leigh, it would get whomever went in search of him; most likely Cdr. Leigh was just out collecting his thoughts.

"As long as they're all in one place," said the Russian. No sooner had he uttered these words than Leigh came into camp.

"No one told me where you'd be," he said.

"My goodness, that's true," said Giacomo, with a forced laugh. "We sure are sorry, aren't we?"

"It's not so funny," said Nkeida.

"Did you find water?" asked Giacomo.

"Yeah," said Leigh. He sat down in the dust and said nothing more. Supper was prepared, and after the meal the six explorers settled back in silence, each occupied by his own thoughts.

Benarcek thought about the lack of wonder he felt, the emptiness where he had expected a kind of glory. Part of it was the loneliness, the alienation. He couldn't pick up a telephone and call his mother or his sister and talk about what he had done. And he hadn't done anything except look at a few rocks and sneeze a lot. This was Jennings's World. It looked like a large park, a large, empty, quiet park.

Leigh thought about how much he wanted to hit Carolyn Giacomo, with a rock, probably. But he knew that if he tried, he would end up with his neck broken and Giacomo standing over him, laughing. He had carried a woman across the arid wastes of Mars. He had saved that woman's life, even if he did make her hate him in the process. And now it was as if Leigh had been nothing, forever nothing, and Carolyn Giacomo was reveling in that knowledge. Leigh wanted to show her what he really was. He was determined to do that, as soon as possible. Just the way he had shown that woman on Mars.

Nkeida thought about her home and her family. Her parents had been failures. When Judy Swan Nkeida was granted a doctorate by virtue of her accomplishments, rather than by fulfilling a regular course of study, her mother had reacted scornfully. Judy Swan Nkeida almost began looking at her degree as a failure, too. And now, if this planet proved to be uninhabited, as it seemed, she would be able to do nothing. Nothing. A failure. And her throat still hurt.

Carolyn Giacomo was enjoying herself. She didn't care what happened. This is what she liked doing. She could have been in Indonesia or Honduras. It looked kind of like the places she had fought in. All that was lacking was an enemy. And if one failed to materialize, there were always Engerev and Leigh.

The Russian thought about his wife and his children. They had already lived without him for four years. They had either adjusted to his absence or they had not. There was nothing to be done in either case. That pleased

81

Engerev, and it made him uncomfortable. He was just beginning to feel expendable. He had been replaced, either by another man, another husband, another father; or, worse, he had been replaced by absolutely nothing. He wasn't necessary. He had never been necessary.

Ajez waited. He hoped that nothing serious would happen. There was no one to consult. He had little confidence. He wanted to go back to Yucatan as quickly as possible. He wanted to treat children's diseases in small towns. He wanted to go to his office on streets filled with goats and sheep. In eighteen months, he would go back to sleep and wake up at home. If he kept his spiritual eyes closed that long, everything would be all right.

The night deepened; in the stillness, the six heard the first sounds from the planet's creatures. Insects and birds, probably. Cheepings and buzzings and distant raucous calls. It meant animal life. It meant hope for the project.

"Engerev, you keep first watch," said Giacomo. "Two hours. Then wake up Leigh. Two hours, then Leigh wakes up Benarcek. Then Ajez. Then we get up and have breakfast."

"Here, take the pistol," said Benarcek, handing the weapon across the smoldering embers to Engerev.

"Thanks," said the Russian. "I'll slaughter them all if they so much as look at me cross-eyed."

"Who?"

"They," said Engerev. "There's always a they."

"Well," said Giacomo, "give 'em one for me." She curled herself beneath the light plastic blanket she carried in her pack and went to sleep. The others did likewise.

A rustling of the grasses that surrounded the rocky area woke Benarcek with a start. He looked out into the darkness; the fire had died down, and Leigh was sleeping at his guard post. Benarcek stared into the dimness, but all that he could see was a vague outline of hills on the horizon and a sky with crystal-sharp stars burning brightly. The rustling came again. "The wind," said Benarcek to himself. "Isn't that what they always tell themselves? 'Only the wind.' I'd better wake Cdr. Leigh up." Dr. Benarcek stood up sleepily and walked the few yards to Leigh's still dark shape. "Commander Leigh," he said.

Leigh woke up, startled. "What's the matter?"

"You were asleep."

"Oh." Leigh stood up and checked the pistol. "Thanks. How much longer before you relieve me?"

Benarcek looked at the glowing dial of his watch. "About another hour and a quarter," he said. "You've only been out here forty-five minutes."

"And I was asleep already. Don't tell anybody, okay?"

"Sure," said Benarcek. "No harm done."

"Thanks," said Leigh. He was prevented from saying anything more by the same rustling noise that had wakened Benarcek.

"Listen," said Benarcek. "I heard that before."

"I'll check it out," said Leigh. He walked slowly and silently toward the source of the noise. There was nothing but quiet and darkness for a moment; then Leigh switched on a portable lamp. Benarcek gasped; a naked man was caught by surprise against the rock wall. He was tall and slender, filthy, covered with mud dried on his arms and legs, excrement matting his hair, leaves and twigs twisted in his beard. He seemed to be about twenty-five to thirty years old, the victim of dietary deficiencies. He raised one hand to his eyes and stood before them, shivering slightly.

"There he is," said Benarcek, his voice full of pity, "our good neighbor across the vast gulf of space."

"He looks like a candidate for electrotherapy," said Leigh. "What do we do with him?"

"We take him into camp, feed him something, then tie him up. This is Dr. Nkeida's territory, now." Benarcek stared at the terrified man for a moment. "You can put your pistol down, Leigh. He isn't armed."

A few minutes later, Benarcek and Leigh had aroused the others and introduced the naked man as the planet's first example of indigenous human life forms on the planet. Carolyn Giacomo was scornful. Dr. Nkeida was excited but a little frightened. Sanchito Ajez gave the man a quick examination and arrived at the same conclusions that Benarcek had; the native showed the results of many years of limited and unsatisfactory diet. His skeletal frame was bent by the lack of calcium and phosphorus in his diet; the trend would continue until the man's old age, when he would be a virtual cripple.

Ajez estimated that old age in the kind of primitive sub-human group the man represented might mean forty years, if the individual hadn't fallen prey to any number of dangerous factors in the environment before that time. The people would be subject to a staggering number of diseases, many of which would be fatal but that caused only minor annoyance to the people of Earth. Measles, for instance, or influenza, could wipe out whole tribes.

"So we guard him until morning," said Giacomo. "I want to go back to sleep."

"Aren't you at all curious?" asked Engerev.

"Curious?" said the woman. "About what? We already found what we're looking for. Let's go home. Or at least back to sleep."

Leigh supervised Ajez and Benarcek as they tied up the native, who sat through the whole procedure shaking with fear but making no movements or sounds. Then, following Giacomo's advice, they all tried to go back to sleep.

At dawn, Giacomo was the first to wake up. She stood, stretching, and stared across the plain. There was no movement except the constant, eternal waving of the grasses. She went to the guard post and found Ajez asleep. She kicked his shoulder lightly and he woke up. "What's wrong?" he asked.

"While you were asleep, some huge carnivore walked into the camp and killed Nkeida, Benarcek, and Leigh," said Giacomo.

"What?" cried Ajez, horrified. "Why didn't I hear anything?"

"You're a sound sleeper," said the weapons expert. "It was a very quiet carnivore."

"There wasn't any animal," said Ajez.

"There could have been," said Giacomo.

"What about that ape man that was crawling around here last night?"

"He's still tied up. He never went to sleep."

"He's a real animal for you. I hate to touch him, even just to take his pulse."

"He's a whole lot better than some of the men on this mission," said Giacomo cynically, as she turned away and went back to the campsite. Ajez stood up and followed her angrily.

Judy Swan Nkeida was giving instructions to the party. She didn't want this first contact spoiled, even though it was already definitely contaminated by the way the native had been captured and bound. "No one says anything to him but me," said Dr. Nkeida. "No one feeds him. No one even looks at him. I'm going to try to establish communication with the subject, and I don't need extraneous factors muddying up my data."

"I know that if I were sitting in a bunch of nutty-looking people like us, tied up hand and foot, I wouldn't be inclined to react with simple objectivity," said Leigh.

"That's because you're civilized," said Nkeida. "He's much simpler. He'll do anything to insure that we won't kill him and that he'll be fed."

"You mean just because he's naked and he's dirty you've decided that he's not civilized?" asked Engerev.

Nkeida sighed. She didn't want to have to explain everything she knew about anthropology and sociology. "What do you mean by 'civilized'?" she asked. "What do you mean by 'dirty'?"

"What do you mean by 'naked'?" said Leigh with a quick leer.

Nkeida ignored him and sat down beside the native. She held a flat plastic plate with some boiled rations on it before the man.

"If I were him, I wouldn't know that was food," said Ajez. "In fact, I didn't until the second week of orientation in Australia."

Nkeida ate a forkful of the food. Then she put a forkful against the tightly closed lips of the native. He opened his mouth and swallowed the food, making a displeased expression.

"He seems to be normal," said Ajez.

"Food," said Nkeida. She waited in vain for the native to repeat the word. She pointed to herself and said, "Judy." She pointed to the man and waited. He said nothing.

"Maybe his mother taught him not to speak to strangers," said Giacomo.

"Shut up," said Nkeida. She pointed to herself again

and repeated her name. Then she touched the man's hairy chest with her forefinger and waited. Again, there was only silence.

"I'll try again later," said Nkeida. "In the meantime, I don't want anybody interfering with this native."

"How do you *interfere* with somebody?" asked Giacomo.

"Step into my office and you'll find out," said Cdr. Leigh. Giacomo turned to him and bit her thumb in a gesture of contempt.

"We're just going to watch his reactions for a few hours," said Dr. Nkeida. "Untie his hands."

Major Engerev complied with the order. Everyone moved away, pointedly ignoring the savage. Nkeida watched him carefully; he did not move for several minutes. Nkeida put a double handful of small twigs on the smoldering embers of the cooking fire; they caught fire and blazed up. The native made a stifled cry of fear and backed away, his hand in front of his eyes again.

"Well," said Giacomo, "they don't know about fire."

"That puts them kind of low on the old scale," said Leigh.

"If they're a nomadic kind of folk," said Nkeida impatiently, "and they live on fruit and wild roots and tubers, they don't need fire. That doesn't mean that they're culturally unsophisticated."

Nkeida watched his activities for the rest of the morning, offering him various things to touch and examine. He did not appear to know what to do with a heavy branch, either as a club or a tool to break the shells of some nuts gathered from low trees in the area. When given a cupful of water, the man put his hand into it and rubbed a few drops across his forehead. He looked at the cup closely, not noticing that he was spilling the water until half of it had soaked into the dry dirt of the campsite. He bent down low and licked the moist dust, instead of drinking the remaining water in the cup.

"Less than promising," said Benarcek. "But still interesting."

"Ask this Neanderthal about the radio beacon," said Engerev.

"Yeah," said Leigh to the aborigine, "what about the beacon?"

"I said no one was to speak to him," said Dr. Nkeida, barely able to control her rage.

"What difference does it make?" asked Leigh. "He wouldn't understand if I hit him across the head with a rock."

Leigh's words, unfortunately, seemed to be the truth. After a while, Nkeida decided that she was making no progress at all in communicating with the native. "Untie the rest of the ropes," she said. "I planted a tracing bug in his hair. We'll be able to follow him. If we lose him, we'll find someone else. If his whole tribe seems to be as unpromising as he is, we'll move to a different part of the continent. I'll want to sample the inhabitants of the whole continent, and then the people on the other continents. It may be that this man is a special case, an outcast madman, perhaps. Or his tribe might not be representative. It's too early to make any scientific judgments." Benarcek untied the man, but the native did not move.

"Is he too stupid to know that he's free?" asked Giacomo.

" 'Stupid' is a loaded word," said Nkeida.

"I meant it to be," said Giacomo.

"Let's just watch what he does," said the black anthropologist.

The naked man watched the fire intently for a few moments, until the flames died down. Nkeida tossed another handful of sticks onto the fire, and it burned brightly again. The man jumped back, but he crept slowly closer as the fire shrank. He picked up a couple of twigs that Nkeida had dropped, and put them in the fire. He held his hands over the flames, too closely, and he grimaced in pain. He still didn't make a sound, though.

"He's playing with fire," said Giacomo. "Most kids would be punished for that."

"I think it's a sign of inherent intelligence," said Benarcek. "He's already using what we've shown him. He's experimenting. Aren't I right, Dr. Nkeida?"

"It looks that way," she said. "He might burn himself up in the process, but he's showing more aptitude and interest than a lower creature would."

"Well," said Engerev, "what do you think?"

Nkeida made an impatient gesture. "What do you want me to do? Do you think I can make conclusions from a couple of hours of observation? Don't be silly. If I showed you a photograph of a single star, could you tell me the latitude and longitude of the place where the camera was?"

Engerev was annoyed. "I just wanted your opinion, not an argument. Is this guy a special case? Is he typical of what we might find here?"

"How do I know?" said Nkeida.

"He's playing with fire," said Giacomo. "Most kids "Ask her how she got her degree," said Giacomo, sneering. "That always gets her mad."

"The subject looks like he's ready to leave," said Ajez.

Sure enough, the man was furtively walking along the low rock cliffs, trying to slip away unnoticed while the research team argued among themselves.

"Let him go," said Nkieda. "That's what we want him to do. Now he'll lead us to his friends."

"I'll give you five to two he leads us to a smelly cave and a half-eaten corpse of a sheep," said Leigh.

"Do they have sheep here?" said Engerev innocently. Leigh just gave the Russian a threatening look.

"We'll stay about a quarter of a mile behind him, moving at his pace. I don't think we'll be spotted. I want a long, undisturbed look at his community. At nightfall, I'll go with Giacomo and Ajez to the outer boundaries of the community, and leave about a half-dozen small tape units. That way, after about a week or so, we can have complete records of everything that was said or done there; the computers can sift it all for me. Benarcek, that will be your job, I guess. We won't have to endanger the objectivity of our data, and we'll get a much more complete and accurate picture."

They sat around the fire, waiting. They could hear the progress of the native as he broke twigs and pushed through grass on his way home. There was no sense in following him yet; Nkeida's tracing device was sending out signals inaudible to people—Nkeida never mentioned that it might be wrong to assume the signals were inaudible to this savage of Jennings's World but recorded and plotted on a small, hand-held receiver. They didn't want to take the chance of being seen by the native and having him bolt in the wrong direction.

After about fifteen minutes Dr. Nkeida nodded, and the others gathered up their things and started along the path the man had made through the high growth. Wolf 359 was beaming hot summertime rays down upon them, through a magenta-tinged sky. The air was still and stifling. There were no sounds during the day, no birds or insects. Only human beings were about through the uncomfortable weather.

The native had left an easily readable path; the tracing bug was almost unnecessary. Behind the rock wall the plain continued unbroken to the horizon. A narrow swath of trampled weeds showed where the man had gone. Carolyn Giacomo insisted on leading the way, armed with one of her guns, but Judy Swan Nkeida remarked that in this situation she knew more about what was happening, so Nkeida led the party, and Giacomo guarded their otherwise unprotected back.

They walked through the grass for nearly an hour. The growth was almost unbearably irritating; the strange plants made the humans' eyes water and throats itch. Even with Dr. Ajez's preventive inoculations, they were driven to the verge of nausea and dizziness. They stumbled forward, blindly, unhappily. Finally, though, Dr. Benarcek, second in the party, bumped suddenly into Nkeida, who raised a warning hand.

"We're here," she said.

Benarcek and the others looked, curious and excited. Before them, in a large area of prairie grass and low trees, about twenty-five or thirty humans were resting in the sparse shade.

"The community," said Nkeida.

"And they all look a lot like our midnight visitor," said Engerev. "So he wasn't an outcast."

"Unless all of these are outcasts," said Leigh.

"Quiet," said Nkeida. "We don't want to give our presence away. We're going to have to be completely silent and invisible until it gets dark."

"Eight hours," said Leigh sourly. "I don't feel like it."

"Then go home," said Nkeida.

"Wouldn't you love it if I did?" said Leigh, grinning. All of the others had a sudden, terrifying picture of how simple it would be for any member of the group to return to the shuttle, open it and begin its computer-guided operation, lift off to the *Unexpected Guest*, and program the mother ship to return to Earth. Any of them could do that at any time.

It wasn't only the tribe of aborigines that had to be watched. Leigh's remark gave them all another full-time hobby.

Benarcek watched the tribe of human creatures with little interest. He would rather have gotten down to the cut-and-dried labor of processing the information; he wished that he didn't have to go through the tedious procedure of gathering that information.

Engerev observed the tribe coldly, without any of the enthusiasm that might have been expected after so long an indoctrination and the dangers of the journey. But, in one sense, he had just come along for the ride, he had already done his job in getting them on the planet, and he resented having to do any more work until it was time to go home.

Nkeida, of course, was so excited that it was nearly impossible for her to carry out her duties properly. Her main struggle was to keep objectivity in her interpretation of information, a struggle that was made more difficult by the carelessness of her associates. She had to restrain some of them who wanted to rush in and establish the space voyagers' superiority, and she had to labor to encourage those who didn't care at all. She wondered how either group had gotten past the psych board, but then she realized that none of her fellow explorers were at all stupid. They just didn't care about the mission the way she did.

Carolyn Giacomo really didn't care, in much the way that Engerev didn't care. As a weapons and military expert, she was glad to have the chance to use her theoretical knowledge, something that had rarely happened on Earth, where most conflicts were resolved by the timidity of the populace. Here on Jennings's World, Giacomo hoped to participate in a full-scale battle. Just once, she thought, just once she'd like to stand at the front of her forces and challenge another belligerent party. She conveniently forgot that the savages of Jennings's World hardly represented a military power.

Dr. Sanchito Ajez had a great deal of scientific curiosity; he felt that studying the people of Wolf 359, in their natural and vulnerable state, would give the people on Earth a great deal of information about their own history. He wanted to see how much natural immunity the aborigines had, and what health precautions they had developed. He wished that Dr. Nkeida hadn't forbidden him and the others to enter the humanoid settlement until she had observed it. Without that study to occupy him, he felt next to useless.

Cdr. Leigh had few emotional responses to the situation. He was killing time until the scientists had finished their studies. At least the climate on Wolf 359's planet was more hospitable than that of Mars. If something happened, he wouldn't have to do without food and water. If something happened, he decided as he looked around the cluster of curious explorers, he wouldn't carry any of them more than about a hundred yards.

"If that's what the people here are like," said Giancomo, "our jobs are going to be pretty easy. I think we'll just take a few tapes and leave. Maybe Ajez here could thump some chests, just to see if they had hearts and stuff. Otherwise I don't see why we can't be on our way home by . . . oh, maybe lunchtime tomorrow."

"I've explained my search schedule," said Nkeida. "We'll go on to some other part of the continent tomorrow. This group could be the one backward tribe on the world. We might have landed in an unfortunate area; what if someone came to Earth and set down in Africa somewhere?"

"What of it?" asked Cdr. Leigh suspiciously. "You're from Niamey yourself."

"That's what I mean," said Nkeida angrily. "I know what I'm talking about. Just because you're black, too, don't think that you know what it's like to grow up hungry."

"I grew up in Rhodesia," said Leigh.

"Let's leave the biographical sketches out of this," said Engerev.

"I was trying to make a point," said Nkeida.

91

"Fine, fine," said Benarcek. "And we agree." He looked at Giacomo, who was staring in disgust at the tribe of humanoid primitives.

"They're pretty damn stupid," said Ajez.

"How can you tell?" asked Nkeida, trying desperately to protect her small area of authority.

"Just look at them."

"A baby on Earth wouldn't live any better," said Nkeida. "Would you say they were all stupid?"

"Now you're playing semantics," said Engerev. "Besides, these aren't babies. They're adults, and I don't think a single one of them has ever even used a branch as a club or as a lever to move something. An interstellar beacon is beyond their means, wouldn't you agree, Dr. Nkeida?"

She frowned. "Yes, Major, I agree."

"Let's go home," said Giacomo.

The mission was starting off somewhat differently than the Earth-based computers had planned.

While the observers argued among themselves, the man whom they had captured the night before walked into the middle of the tribe, waving his hands and uttering hoarse grunting noises.

"Listen," said Benarcek. "He's trying to communicate with the others."

"Sure," said Giacomo. "It's the five o'clock report. He's the anchorman of Jennings's World."

The man spent a few minutes wildly gesturing and bellowing. None of the other tribespeople seemed to appreciate what he was doing; the children moved away from him and started picking up stones. The man saw that he was not getting through; he went to a low, twisted tree and gathered a double handful of dry twigs from the dead limbs. He placed these on the ground in a pile, much like the sticks on the fire in the explorers' camp. He waved his hand over the sticks, expecting them to burst into flame as the others had. They did not. He tried again, making low hissing sounds at the sticks. The people of his tribe turned away, either bored or concerned with the more important matter of collecting a meager meal from the sparse vegetation of the area.

"He wants a fire," said Nkeida. "That demonstrates conclusively that he assimilated what happened to him in our camp. He remembered our fire and he's trying to reproduce it here. That proves a certain level of intelligence."

"How many points does he lose for the way he's going about it?" asked Giacomo.

"Do you mean these people don't have fire?" asked Ajez.

"Sure," said Engerev. "Lots of things don't have fire. Lizards don't have fire. Trees don't have fire, except after storms. It puts these people closer to their surroundings. They are more of an organic part of their environment. Fire is an intruder."

"Give them fire," said Cdr. Leigh, "and the next thing you know, they'll be wanting frying pans."

"That's the idea," said Nkeida. "I sort of feel sorry for them."

"They have to live out their poor lives without rigatoni," said Giacomo. "Just think."

"What should we do?" asked Benarcek.

"Watch," said Nkeida. "Listen. Record. That's all."

"I took an oath to help people," said Ajez. "I don't know if I can just watch these primitives without trying to help them a little."

"How do you know you'd be helping them?" asked Nkeida. "All you'd be doing is imposing your standards on them. It might be like putting brassieres on pet dogs. They may have existed exactly like this for thousands of years. If there were anything wrong with it, they would have changed."

"So according to your line of thought," said Engerev, "this is the best of all possible worlds for them. Otherwise, they'd have chosen something else. And the same goes for us. We live in the best possible way, because if it weren't, we'd choose something else. Do you really believe that?"

"No," said Nkeida.

"It sounded good for a few seconds there," said Giacomo.

"Then you agree that we have a kind of responsibility to help them out," said Benarcek.

"No, no," said Nkeida. "I want to observe them just as they are."

"You want to keep them ignorant and diseased, just for the sake of your reputation back on Earth," said Cdr. Leigh, leaving the group of explorers and walking slowly toward the aborigines. As soon as the natives saw him, they started behaving in a terrified manner. They growled and threw dirt and stones at Leigh. The commander did not hesitate. Some of the natives ran away; some were too confused to move. Their former captive crouched over his dead pile of twigs. Leigh walked up to him, bent down, took out a pocket lighter, and set the sticks on fire. The native scuttled backward quickly, making soft mewing sounds. Leigh stayed motionless after he lit the fire. The man whom the exploration team had captured crept closer to the flames, and passed his hand through them.

"He does that a lot," said Engerev. "He must really enjoy pain."

"Leigh, get back here!" cried Nkeida. The black man ignored her.

The native made strange noises and waved to his tribe. Slowly they gathered around him and stared silently at the fire.

"All right, kids," said Cdr. Leigh, "you've got the fire. Play with it a while and then we'll pass out merit badges." He turned around and walked back to his fellows. The savages didn't react to his leaving; they came slowly closer to the fire.

"That's really wonderful," said Nkeida. She looked crushed. Her experiment and her plans for the book she would write about it seemed destroyed by Leigh's thoughtless action. Nkeida could see only failure. Ajez might successfully fulfill his rôle on the team. Giacomo still might, if hostile natives were encountered. Benarcek certainly would; he would have to collate and code data, no matter how contaminated it might be. Leigh himself had already performed his assignment, as had Engerev. Only Nkeida depended on the human life forms themselves, and now her programmed research had been hopelessly ruined. There was no longer any chance for objectivity. Her report would have to begin, "If Cdr Leigh had not interfered . . ." What would be the conclusion? What validity would it have? None, absolutely none. It would all be speculation. And that, in the eyes of her fellow scientists, was failure.

"Look," said Benarcek. Nkeida looked where he pointed, through a blurring of her own tears. She saw that some of the natives had thrust sticks into the fire and were watching them burn. One woman held a dry, blazing branch like a torch. It was burning very close to her hand, and in a very short while she would learn an important characteristic of fire.

"Can't you use that?" asked Engerev.

"Sure, sure," said Nkeida. "We'll plant the recording devices anyway. After all, the people at home paid for them."

The natives had all dropped their burning sticks. Looks of fear and awe were on their faces. Slowly they raised their eyes from the flames to where the Earth scientists stood. One young man pointed at Leigh. The others stumbled backward a few feet, muttering their unintelligible noises. The savage who had been captured pointed at Leigh. Others raised their hands in his direction.

"They like me," said Leigh.

"You know what," said Giacomo, laughing, "I really think you've given them more than just fire. I think you've just invented religion on Jennings's World."

"Am I a god?" asked Leigh.

"I'll bet you are," said Engerev. "Anyway, you have all the qualifications. You stand pretty high in the arbitrariness ratings."

"That fire was a miracle," said Benarcek. "Now they probably want you to feed them."

"Let them eat sticks," said Leigh. "And why don't we go back to camp? I'm hungry, too."

"And the divine revelation sinks slowly in the west," said Giacomo. "They've probably never seen a black man before. They probably think that you're Engerev's shadow or something."

"The Great Black God from Beyond the Stars," said Leigh. "And his beautiful black wife." He smiled at Nkeida, an ugly, demeaning smile; the sociologist shuddered and looked away.

"Well," said Engerev, "we're going back to the camp.

Why don't one of you gods ask them about the beacon?"

"Let's leave that until they evolve a bit," said Leigh. "At least a couple of centuries. I don't want to be cheated out of my palace and pyramid."

"All right," said Benarcek. "But if you get to be a god, I get to be one, too."

"Sure," said Leigh, yawning. "I'm as generous and just as they come."

"I know just what, too," murmured Nkeida. Leigh glanced at her but didn't say anything. They watched the savages for a moment more, then turned and recrossed the prairie to their campsite.

As they waded through the high grass, Dr. Justin Benarcek was aware of muttered conversations behind him. Ahead of him there was Engerev, who seemed always to be trying to assume an authority to which he had no claim. The Russian was a major, of course, but that did not mean so very much, especially in the cooled-down military world they had left. Engerev was a Russian, and he was alone. Perhaps Nkeida could give Benarcek a better rationale for Engerev's behavior. Leigh was certainly no puzzle, other than the way he had rigged his profiles to pass the review boards. Leigh was dangerous. He had already spoiled the authenticity of Dr. Nkeida's results. The others—

The others. Eighteen months with the others. Benarcek shuddered.

A few days later, Dr. Nkeida had enough tapes to make a preliminary judgment. "Social systems are related to biological systems," she said. "If you give these people an environment that's stable, as this one seems to be, then there is no reason to expect them to change beyond it, unless the species itself is changed. But look at us, at our culture. Aspects of our culture change all the time, even with a stable environment."

"So giving them fire was a good thing," said Leigh defensively.

"No," said Nkeida. "Not yet."

"Prove it," said Leigh.

"Call fire a tool," said Nkeida.

"All right. Fire is a tool," said Engerev.

"Captain," said Giacomo sourly.

"Now why did some of our ancestors' ancestors use fire, and the rest of them stayed up in the trees eating eggs?" asked the woman. No one answered. "Because the ones that dropped out of the trees didn't have to hang onto branches any longer. Their hands were free. Now these humanoids on this world spend their time in an analogous activity, brushing aside the tall grass that covers most of their territory. If they didn't have to do that, they might have developed tools before now. They are not fit socially to have tools and the anthropological benefits that go with them."

"Are you going to take the fire back?" asked Leigh forget about it."

"It's too late," said Nkeida. "I can hope that they'll contemptuously.

"I doubt it," said Benarcek.

"So do I," said Nkeida. "But these tapes are going into the shuttle ship, and into the *Guest*, and it won't be my skin when we get home."

"Should I make a comment about your skin?" asked Giacomo. "Or do we count that as a given?"

"Let's skip it tonight, Lieutenant Giacomo," said Leigh, his teeth bared in an evil grin.

"Carolyn," said Leigh. Giacomo just turned around and stepped into the deeping shadows.

"What now, Dr. Nkeida?" asked Dr. Benarcek a little while later. They were both sitting up, staring at the stars in the clear night sky.

"I want to go somewhere else, somewhere where Leigh hasn't spoiled my data. I'd like to try a part of the continent where the grass wasn't so common that people's lives are spent brushing it away. Then we'd find people who have to supplement their diets with meat. That means killing. That means tools. That means cultural activity and a premium on intelligence."

Benarcek was already asleep.

PART FOUR

2022

CHAPTER 6

Commander Leigh stood by the side of the shuttle craft. The remainder of the research team was still asleep at its camp. The air was chill, and Leigh's fingers were stiff. He set the combination locks in the proper sequence and was rewarded with the sudden humming of the shuttle craft's return to life. In a few moments, a door opened in the side of the craft, and Cdr. Leigh entered.

He went straight for the control section of the shuttle craft. He closed the door, buckled himself into his seat, shut the outside hatch, and lifted off the grass plateau. He raised the shuttle craft a distance of no more than twenty-five feet. He circled it around, watching through the view ports to see whether anyone had heard him or followed him in the pre-dawn darkness. He saw no one. His expression was solemn. He did not gloat over what he was about to do. He did not conjure plans in his mind or pretend what the reactions of the others might be. Commander Leigh was a very practical man.

He burned off an area of the plain about a hundred yards in diameter around the settlement of the humanoids, using the heat projector mounted amidships. The burning went quickly. There was little fire, just a blackening of the brush and plant life, a burning of the soil where the grasses had grown. The sound awoke the humanoids; the noises were transmitted back through Dr. Nkeida's instruments, some of which were also destroyed, but Cdr. Leigh did not care. He returned the shuttle to its former position, closed it up again, locked it, and returned to the campsite.

The affair had also wakened his colleagues, all of whom waited for Leigh's explanation. Nkeida was crying openly. Engerev and Benarcek looked angry. Giacomo was curious. Ajez was confused.

"Next step," said Leigh simply, lying down to resume his interrupted night's sleep. "It was obvious. Now their food-gathering has to change."

Nkeida collapsed, sobbing.

"Shut up, Judy," murmured Leigh. "Think of it as a dynamic assignment. Watch what happens, not what happened before you got here."

There were no longer fruits or nuts to eat from the low trees which Leigh had burned without a trace. Whatever roots and vegetables grew in the grassy growth were likewise gone. The natives were angry and horrified. Most of the research team felt the same. Cdr. Leigh, however, stepped forward confidently. He chose the same fellow who had followed them back to their campsite; he beckoned, and the aborigine followed. "This guy must be the Leonardo da Vinci of his peer group," said Leigh.

Leigh and the native, whom the team members had named Adam, waited at the edge of the burned-off area. After several minutes, Leigh saw something moving within the grass. It might have been another member of the native community, but that thought did not occur to Leigh until afterward. Using a handgun, Leigh killed the small animal, had Adam carry it back to the community, where Leigh showed him how to skin and dress the creature. Making another fire, Leigh cooked the meat and gave some to each member of the native community.

"That smells better than anything we've had to eat in days," complained Benarcek.

The natives grabbed the food and ate it quickly. Some were hesitant. Others, after eating the meat and thinking about where it had come from, vomited it up again. But on the whole, the plan was successful. Lacking the handguns, of course, and the firemaking apparatus, the people of Jennings's World would have to learn alternative methods, ones more in keeping with their almost non-existent technological level.

"They're starting a language, you'll notice," said Nkeida glumly. "They say two words. They say 'fire' and they say 'Leigh'."

"He has a lot of take-charge ability," said Ajez. "Are you certain that you feel all right?"

"I want to go home," said Nkeida.

The next day, Leigh showed Adam and two of the other adult humanoids that if they sat together near the edge of the burned area, they could see the movements of animals within the still-standing grasses. Leigh demonstrated the idea of the club to them, and with great and gleeful success the humanoids killed enough food to last them another day.

"They learn fast," said Leigh. "You should make a note of that."

Nkeida took out a small pocket communicator. "Nkeida to info storage. They learn fast. Over."

"Get into the spirit of the thing," said Leigh. "There's a lot of work to be done."

"Call me when you want to invent the Queen of the Nile," she said, turning angrily and walking away.

"Touchy," said Ajez. "In eighteen months, I doubt if we could move them through the old Stone Age."

"I wonder if we ought to," asked Benarcek.

"A pointless thought," said Giacomo. "I'm still waiting to divide up into teams."

"Next Wednesday, about two o'clock," said Leigh, slapping Giacomo's back. The weapons officer looked darkly at the commander, as though she wanted to cut his hand off. Leigh laughed. That seemed to be the common attitude to take in order to relieve tension. To Benarcek, it seemed less and less healthy.

Commander Leigh demonstrated the club, the bludgeon, the spear, and the bow and arrow to the humanoids. At first, the humanoids preferred the one-on-one quality of the club, but were dismayed by the fleetness of the quarry. This led to a dissatisfaction with the weapons system, and a quick appreciation of the spear and the bow and arrow. This was a major leap upward in social progress, according to the now-dispirited Nkeida. Captain Carolyn Giacomo watched with approval.

"I've been thinking about these people," said Benarcek the following day. "They couldn't come close to being as stupid as we found them. It's as if they had all the necessary biosocial requirements, but never received whatever impetus pushed our ancestors."

"There," declared Cdr. Leigh triumphantly to Dr. Nkeida, "there's the thesis for your new study. Why these people hadn't been prodded before now, and the remarkable progress they're making once we did give them a shove. Call it: 'Man or Unman: The Making of a Race.' Give me a footnote."

"She'll give you the foot, all right," said Giacomo, putting her arm around Nkeida's quivering shoulders. "And I'll take over when she's through. And you know where those kicks are aimed."

"Just a thought," said Leigh, shrugging.

"You know, that's an interesting idea," said Dr. Benarcek. "This may be finally the clue we've needed to understand our own development. But the idea of a single event triggering the intellectual and social consciousness of a race is hard to accept."

"You can see for yourself," said Engerev. "What were those brutes doing before we arrived? They were eating dirt and whatever nutritious vegetable matter happened to go along with it. Now they've become hunters. This afternoon I saw a man scraping a piece of stone into a knife, to skin his kill better. Toolmaking. There's a universe of difference between that and the simple lever-use of undeveloped apes."

"A universe of difference," said Dr. Ajez, unaccountably shivering.

"They're progressing at remarkable speed," said Nkeida thoughtfully. "Whoever would have thought it possible?"

"I did," said Leigh carelessly. "Otherwise, I never would have shown them fire."

"Don't be pompous about your mistakes," said Engerev.

"Mistakes?" cried Leigh angrily. "At least I don't go off to Earth and let them grow old and die behind me." Engerev's eyes grew wide, then he leaped at the black commander. They wrestled on the ground for several minutes, fruitlessly, until each was out of breath. Then they stood, panting, facing each other.

"We're all going to know everything about everybody," said Nkeida sadly. "And to think how much I valued privacy."

"You didn't value privacy," said Giacomo viciously. "You just wanted to be special. And you never were very special, were you? Look how you've ruined this assignment already."

"I've had some help," said the frail black sociologist.

"How would you like to come watch an example of the fine field work I've done in the wake of your catastrophe?" asked Leigh.

"That's not a very tactful way of putting it," said Benarcek.

"Does 'tact' have much survival value?" asked Leigh.

"It does, when your words are directed at Judy Swan," said Carolyn Giacomo. "We're reaching an understanding."

"What were you so anxious to show us?" asked Ajez.

"Our gang has moved through the Paleolithic to the old Stone Age and further, I think. Come on. We can watch an organized hunt."

"Isn't it a little late in the day to start a hunt?" asked Benarcek.

"That's one of the main points," said Leigh. "My friend Adam has divided his fellows up into bow-men, spear-men, and club-men, and they're going out on their first hunt at dusk."

"Dusk?"

"Wait and see," said Leigh.

Nkeida only shook her head. She had been doing a lot of that. And she had been swallowing a lot of Ajez's pills.

Later that day, after darkness had stolen over the plain, Leigh organized his band of prehistoric hunters. Living in close proximity—or reasonably close, having moved off a bit with the arrival of the Earth party—was a variety of natural fauna: lower primates in the low trees and hills around the settlement, marsupials, deerlike animals, doglike animals, and so on. Like the humans, these were day-living, night-sleeping animals. The humans waited

105

well past their usual bedtime and stole forth on the hunt. They smashed the skulls of the primates, stuck deer to the ground with spears, and threw clubs at the awakened dogs. Then began a proud, defiant threefold chant: "Leigh, Leigh, Leigh," and "Food, Food, Food," and "Fire, Fire, Fire." Adam sat in a group of humanoids; together they made a fire and cooked the food. The natives had learned that besides tasting better, cooked food could be kept longer.

"There, Dr. Nkeida, do you know how long it took our ancestors to go from leaf- and berry-eating beasts to hunters?" asked Cdr. Leigh.

"A few million years," said Nkeida gloomily.

"And look what I've wrought in just a few days," said Leigh. "No wonder they think that in some ways I'm like a god. I feel very Promethean, very protective toward these savages. What else do they need?"

"They need quite a bit, depending on whose viewpoint you're taking," said Engerev. "They don't have to wait in long lines yet, not for anything. We could give them the slow-moving checkout counter."

"Don't be stupid," said Leigh. "Can't any of you see the opportunity here? The duty? We owe it to the memory of Dr. Jennings to do what we can for these people."

"Dr. Jennings," sad Benarcek. "These people can't have built that transmitter. Maybe this isn't even the real Jennings's World. It was just the closest."

"It's Jennings's World, now and always," said Leigh. "The other world will have to be explored after we return and make our report. Come on, we have work to do."

"We know that," said Giacomo. "We're just wondering how much that work will look like what we were trained for."

"You'll get your fighting in, don't worry, Carolyn," said Leigh. Giacomo almost slapped the man, but stopped herself. She refused to be baited by him; it was a close thing, though.

After the feast, evidently the first of its kind among the savages, one person after another, man and woman, got up and acted out the part he or she had played in the slaughter of the animals. When the tribe had worked itself up into an emotional frenzy, they began chanting again: Leigh, Leigh, Leigh. The black commander raised his hands to his shipmates and stepped into the dying ember light of the campfire. He faced the savages.

"I know that you won't understand what I'm saying, but I'm proud of you. You've made a very important step toward civilization here today. Civilization is where you belong. I will not return to Earth with the computer-banks filled with data about unwashed, starving natives. Jennings's World will be worth the effort of the people on Earth."

"Leigh! Leigh! Leigh!"

A young woman stepped forward with a cold, half-cooked chunk of meat for him. It was obvious to the Terran crew that along with the offering of food went the offering of the girl as well. Leigh accepted both. The other crew members, disgusted, went back to their camp-site to think about the developments and plan their future courses. Everyone returned but Leigh, who spent the night cushioned from the rock bed of the natives by the soft body of the young, reeking woman.

It was cold in the rocks, and animals could be seen eyeing the natives from the edge of the burned-out area. Leigh realized that these people needed protection. He would give it to them. He would teach them, and they would protect themselves. Surely, no one could blame him for that. What would the report look like if they had to say that all existing inhabitants had been extermi-nated while under the crew's examination?

CHAPTER 7

Dr. Justin Benarcek was more confused than ever. What was their mission? Evidently, to explore the source of the radio beacon, to establish contact with the intelligence that operated it, and maintain friendly relations between the two alien races. Instead, the team from Earth had found nothing more than a pack of near-human animals, none of whom had ever used a lever or an inclined plane to lighten his labor. Well, of course, the truth may be as Dr. Nkeida said; there might be another, more advanced, race somewhere else on the planet. But the beacon was *here*. And, if there were intelligent humans, they'd have listened in on the shuttle craft's communications, would have monitored the *Unexpected Guest* in orbit, and come to meet them. That was a prospect that Benarcek found frightening, that any morning they might wake up to find the sky blazing with airships of the true, proper masters of this world. Then the Earth team would look like fools. They would look like aliens landing on Earth, ignoring the human population, and interviewing the antelopes instead. It might be difficult to explain to the aliens, and to Washington, and to Group One.

Dr. Judy Swan Nkeida was losing her mental equilibrium quickly. Everything that Leigh did was in direct violation of the guidelines of her own job. Everything that man did made her own failure and humiliation that much graver. And fear of failure was Nkeida's primary motivation. She began to withdraw into herself, seeing no help coming from any of the other crew members.

She might as well go back to the mother ship and put herself back into suspended animation. That was a lot like suicide, but not as permanent. There was a lot about the idea that attracted her failing mind.

Carolyn Giacomo, who hadn't run much since the track days of her youth, was already planning how she was going to make off with half of Leigh's aborigine forces and begin her own colony. That was the word that occurred to her mind: colony. And the reason for having colonies, of course, was to encourage warfare. And she'd be leading her somewhat meager troops into battle, against the greedy, rapacious tribespeople of the false god, Leigh . . .

Sanchito Ajez, so far, felt that he was just along for the ride. A couple of pill or dermal dispensers could have served his purpose just as well. As for what Leigh was doing, he had little opinion about it. He wanted the best for everybody. He was sure that it would work out, one way or another.

And Alexei Engerev—the Russian of two minds. He wouldn't be sad to stay with Leigh and become a god in the eyes of the natives, but he had twinges of guilt. He thought of his wife, Ireyn, and the children growing up without him, and he thought that if it were all for something valuable, they might as well all suffer in the interests of science. Leigh was going about his affairs successfully, but less than objectively.

They tried to sleep, but their thoughts prevented drowsiness from overtaking them for some time. It was already getting pink in the east when some of the crew members finally fell asleep.

Not so with Cdr. Leigh and his native wife, whom he named Paula. They had slept well, wrapped in each other's arms. When Leigh awoke, though, his body ached and his back would straighten only after some painful exercising. "We have to do something about this," he muttered.

"Leigh, Leigh," sang Paula.

"Right," said Leigh, yawning. "Leigh. I'll just stand here and wait for breakfast." He pointed to his mouth, and Paula laughed. Leigh shook his head, pointed to his mouth again, and this time Paula understood. She brought him a hard root, which Leigh threw to the ground, and a greasy chunk of marsupial meat, which Leigh gnawed unhappily. "We have so much to accomplish. Agriculture. Architecture. Domestication of animals. It might take all afternoon."

"All afternoon," said Paula.

Leigh stared at her. He had slept with a parrot.

"I wonder if Sanchito has enough soap in his kit for us and you people, too," said Leigh, wrinkling his nose. "Cleanliness has a survival value, unless, of course, stinking too much is even better. I'm not the right person to ask about that."

"Ask about that," said Paula. Leigh patted her naked rear.

By making some motions, Leigh communicated to her that he wanted her to break off a branch from one of the low trees. She did so, and, with his knife and fire-apparatus, he made a sharp, hard point on the stick. "This is a stick," he said, pointing to the stick.

"Stick," said Paula.

"Very good," said Cdr. Leigh. "Stick."

"This is a stick," said Paula. Leigh only stared again. Where had she picked up the grammar? And the words? The natives had heard a good deal of discussion the previous day. Perhaps they had—or at least Paula had—a natural affinity for language.

"Now watch," said Leigh. "I'm going to build us a kind of pit hut. No more sleeping on rocks. No more sleeping in the cold." He took the stick and began digging slowly at the hard-packed earth. He chipped it away, bit by bit, until he had dug out a hole about six feet in diameter and a foot deep. "There," he said at last, exhausted. "That's a foundation."

"Hole," said Paula.

Leigh looked at her silently for a long while. "Go get a bunch of branches, longer than these, thinner, to use as a frame for the hut." He did not point or indicate anything. Paula stared, not understanding. "Sticks," he said.

She smiled. "Sticks," she said.

She returned after a few moments with about ten long, slender poles. Leigh dug holes for them and placed them in the ground firmly. Then he bent the poles and planted the other ends in the ground around the perimeter of his round hole. "Now come here," he said to Paula. He led her to the area of the waving grasses. He grabbed some and showed her how to plait rope with it. "Rope," he said when he had made a foot of it.

"Rope," she said.

"Grass," he said, holding his hand up, filled with unwoven grass.

Paula spat disgustedly. It was apparent that her people did not like the grass. It kept them isolated and afraid.

"Grass," said Leigh.

"Yes," said Paula finally. "Grass."

Leigh spread his arms out at great length. "Rope," he said. "Rope. Rope. Rope."

Paula smiled and nodded. She ran to some of the other members of her tribe. Through nods and pointings and the words "Leigh" and "Food," she induced several to help her make rope.

A regular little industrialist, thought Leigh.

Leigh organized a party to find some more marsupials and monkeys for food. While that smaller hunt was going on, the group making rope had finished enough for Leigh's needs. He took some of the stuff, smiling. "Leigh, Leigh," the people chanted.

"Where do you come from?" asked one old woman. Leigh could not reply.

"Rope," said Paula. It was probable, now, that Paula was the dumb one.

Leigh took the rope and bound up the intersections of the bent branches in his hut. Then he threw the skins of the dead animals from the night before over the semicircular construction. "House," said Leigh.

"Our house," said Paula proudly. She held out a hand, and he took it. Together they went inside, and did not emerge for some time. Outside, the natives were chanting "Leigh, Leigh, Leigh," and "Food, Food, Food."

Dr. Nkeida, Capt. Giacomo, Major Engerev, Dr. Benarcek, and Dr. Ajez arrived at the site early the next day and watched as Leigh instructed the primitives in building temporary shelters. They said nothing. They sat crosslegged on the ground, like an audience, watching the purity of their mission dissolving in the brisk, warming air.

After Leigh had finished his hut and gone into it with his native bride, the other humanoids began following his example. They dug holes in the ground about a foot deep, as large around as was necessary to house whatever family units existed. Branches and saplings were bent. Some were soaked in water to make them more pliable. Dr. Nkeida was amazed that this sophistication had come into being without the direction of any of the Earth team. The poles were tied together with plaited grasses, and the whole huts were covered over with sod, plaited mats, or skins. At first there weren't enough skins to go around, so many huts had to be roofed with other things.

"Those skins will be pretty gamy in a day or two," said Engerev. "He doesn't know enough to preserve them better. They should be scraped and scraped, to get all the rotting flesh from them. They should be soaked and dried in the sun. Eskimo women used to chew the skins, for some reason that I've forgotten. But he's made a good start. Instead of the naked tribe of frightened animals we found here, now there's starting to be a kind of village."

"I don't understand," said Dr. Benarcek in some confusion. "Are we condoning what Leigh is doing? Or are we officially against it?"

"How official were the guidelines that we got from Group One on Earth?" asked Giacomo.

"Not very," said Engerev.

"How much against Leigh's progress are you?" asked Ajez.

"Not very," said Engerev. They watched the humanoids building their huts. As a matter of common decency, they tried to ignore the growing sounds of ecstasy coming from Leigh's hut, but it was almost impossible. Paul Drayden Leigh and his Paula brought indulgent smiles to the faces of the humanoids, blushes to the faces of the Earth scientists.

When Leigh and Paula emerged from their hut, the humanoids clapped their hands and hit stones and clubs against the ground. "Food, Food," they chanted. Leigh smiled and walked toward his colleagues. Paula followed. Her speech had rapidly improved, from listening to Leigh's monologues. "Did you come from the grass?" she asked.

"I came from beyond the grass," said Leigh.

"There is no beyond the grass," said Paula, confused.

"Look," said Leigh. He pointed into the clear sky. "That is where I came from."

"That is grass," said Paula. "That is where the grass is all matted and peaceful. It is only down here that it is dangerous and everywhere."

"I come from beyond the grasses," said Leigh. "So do my friends. We came together to meet your people."

Leigh and Paula had joined the silent group of technicians.

"Our god Leigh has told me that you all come from beyond the grass," said Paula. "Is that true?"

"Yes," said Benarcek.

"Do you doubt me?" asked Leigh lightly.

"I doubt them," answered Paula calmly.

"They are my friends," said Leigh.

"I doubt that," said Giacomo softly.

"And did you all come from beyond the grass?" asked Paula.

"Yes, yes, yes," said Engerev.

"It must be wonderful there," said Paula.

"Parking lots, shopping bags with handles that break before you get them home," said Giacomo. "Terrific things like that."

"Do you think that I could ever see this land beyond the grass?" asked Paula. The research team looked at each other. There had been no provision made for returning one of the natives to Earth with them. It had been assumed that if the inhabitants wanted to, they could follow in their own ships, in their own time.

"I think that someday you may see the land we come from," said Cdr. Leigh.

"You mean," said Paula solemnly, "after I die."

"I didn't say that," said Leigh.

"But, great god Leigh, surely that is the only way a person could enter the home of the gods."

"Why don't you try explaining to her again that we're not gods?" asked Nkeida helplessly.

"We're not gods," said Benarcek.

"I see," said Paula. "Only Leigh is a god. It is as I

113

thought." Paula turned and went back to her people, many of whom were still constructing their huts. She spoke with her fellow natives in low tones. After she finished, the savages turned back toward the scientists. "Leigh, Leigh, Leigh," they chanted.

"Kind of reminds you of Mars, doesn't it?" asked Giacomo.

Leigh became furious. "You don't have any idea what happened on Mars," he said.

"No," said the weapons expert, "but we all have a lot of fun thinking about it."

"Well," said Leigh, "are you fellows going to spend another night on the ground tonight? Or are you going to take the suggestion of our poor neighbors here and build some temporary shelters? You have no idea what the climate is like, do you? If it starts to rain, it might not even be water."

"It hasn't hurt them, it seems," said Ajez.

"How do you know?" said Leigh. "They might all be twenty years younger than they look."

"In that case, that girl friend of yours ought to be about two or three," said Benarcek, laughing.

"I just thought about how fast these people are catching on to what we're teaching them," said Nkeida.

"What Leigh's teaching them," said Giacomo.

"Yeah," said Engerev.

"When we found them," said Nkeida, "they were somewhere in a situation analogous to our own Lower Paleolithic age, about two million years ago. In a few days, they've progressed to a level of the Middle Paleolithic, about one hundred thousand years ago. That's one million, nine hundred thousand years' progress in less than a week."

"The thing that most surprises me is their aptitude for our language," said Ajez.

"All these talents, the tool-using, weaponmaking, meat-hunting, shelter-building things, might be latent in man. Before the discovery of just how old man really is, when the church said that Adam was created in 4004 B.C., it was assumed that man came into the world knowing everything he needed to know. There just wasn't an alternative. Man couldn't have learned all of that in just six thousand years," said Nkeida. "Now, though, I don't know what to believe."

"It's possible that these people just aren't typical," said Engerev.

"That's why I want to leave here," said Nkeida.

"That's why I changed the locks on the shuttle craft," said Leigh. "We're staying here. I like being worshipped."

"That wasn't part of the original guidelines," said Benarcek. "We were supposed to stay invisible and record."

"We could have recorded their entire culture in ten minutes," said Leigh. "Now, isn't this more interesting?"

"They're making up for lost time," said Engerev.

"Lost time," said Nkeida wistfully. She got up and started to walk away.

"What are you going to do?" asked Giacomo. Nkeida gave her no answer. Giacomo shrugged.

Paula came back to their group. "We have decided," she said.

"That's always the best way," said Benarcek tiredly.

"Great god Leigh takes those of us whom he chooses with him to the land beyond the grasses, after we have died. There we will spend a long time, until god Leigh tires of us. Then we come back here and begin again. That is why men and women die. That is why children are born."

"Those are answers to questions I've been asking myself since I was a child," said Engerev. "Thank you for letting me in on the truth."

"It is nothing," said Paula coldly.

"Doesn't she like the rest of us?" asked Engerev.

"Just great god Leigh, apparently," said Giacomo.

"Well," said Engerev, "let me at her inside that smelly tent, and I'd show her there's more than one great god around here."

"I have to go now," said Paula. "We are putting together the proper rituals of worship. It is a very difficult thing to do, not yet having any divine revelations to speak of. It will probably be fire and food oriented for the time being." She gazed longingly at Leigh, turned, and left. There was a silence.

"So you changed the combinations, eh?" said Giacomo. "Maybe we can drag the great god away long enough to beat the secret out of him. Even great gods are subject to immediate recall at any moment. I'd like to recall one off the side of his head."

"That's not getting us anywhere," said Engerev. "Maybe we should be taking advantage of the situation and noting it. As odd as it is, it's certainly a new experience for man. We should be drawing up some kind of preliminary ethnography or something."

"The ethnographer is away crying," said Ajez.

That day passed in confusion for the members of the research team. They had been carefully trained for many contingencies during their test period in Australia, but every scenario took as an assumption that the explorers would not come forward and reveal their identities to the natives, not unless it could be proved to the shipboard computer that such a step was warranted. Now everything they had learned and trained for was irrelevant. They could only watch.

After a time, Sanchito Ajez began digging a hole for his own pit hut. He had grown tired of the rough accomodations the scientists had taken. His hut was not far from the village of the humanoids, whom he wanted to begin studying. They didn't seem to be in poor health and, considering their limited diet before Leigh introduced weapons and fire, they were remarkably fit. Adam, the first of the savages caught by the scientists, had gained some social status by that fact, and was now the leader of the great god Leigh cult. Paula was the chief priestess.

Engerev, like Nkeida, just wanted to go home. It wouldn't be quite the amount of time he had planned, but it would be short by only a little over a year. He didn't want to stay around and watch some black pervert become a virtual deity among these backward people.

Benarcek was bemused. His job was to collate data— any data. It made little difference to him what the savages did, as long as the other scientists were recording it. That did not seem to be the case.

Capt. Carolyn Giacomo had plans of her own. She could see the day when she would lead some of these humans off to establish another village. Food would become scarce once the animals had adapted themselves to the savages' new tactics. It would be simple to cause a rift. First a rift, then a rivalry, then open hatred, then warfare . . .

Toward evening Paula came back to where Leigh was sitting. She was carrying some small objects. "These are for you," she said. "We've never done anything like this before, so they might not be very good. I don't know. You're supposed to guide us."

"What are they?"

"Idols, sort of," said Paula. She handed some small carved figurines to Leigh, made from wood and bone. They were stylized human figures, some like clothespins with arms than statues.

"That's another step you've taken. Your people are conceptualizing. Dr. Nkeida would be impressed."

"The black mother of lies?" asked Paula.

"Is that what you call her?"

"Yes." Paula pointed to a particular figurine. It was notable for a gigantic phallus. "This one is you."

"You flatter me," said Leigh, laughing.

"It represents both your sex and the fire. This one is supposed to be me." It looked like some of the primitive fertility symbols found on Earth. It had huge, multiple breasts and a distended belly.

"They didn't do a very good job of capturing you. I like you better the way you are."

Paul smiled. "Thank you. That's supposed to be my soul, though. Together, you and I will create great beings."

"I don't know," said Leigh. "There's no proof that my people and your people can mate."

"What about last night?"

"Oh," said Leigh, "we can go through the motions. But they might not be successful."

"Anyway, it's not 'my people' and 'your people.' It's just you and me. We're special. And I've already proven that I'm not barren."

Leigh couldn't explain to Paula that there might be a chromosomal reason for their not producing offspring. She wouldn't listen to it. "That's nonsense," she said. "A lot of us used to believe that babies came from too much eating. We're wiser now. And what you're saying sounds just as silly."

"I know," said Leigh. "Do you want to try again?"

Paula smiled and, taking the religious figurines, they went into their tent. The ground shook mildly in the neighborhood for half an hour, and when they emerged again, the natives pounded sticks and stones together again. It was becoming a religious festival. Leigh worried about that. If no children developed, whom would they blame? What would they do with the old king? Sacrifice him to the food gods?

The natives—no longer could they be called savages—copied as much of the scientists' ways as they could, even to eating with carved utensils. Every day brought a new revelation of the progress the natives had made. Civilization and culture had only been dormant in these people, and now it woke hungrily. Each member of the community competed with the others to gain attention from the scientists.

"Look," cried Adam one morning. "Come see what I've done today." He dragged Leigh and Engerev with him. They went to the meager pile of rocks that had served the natives as habitation for so many generations until the arrival of the people from Earth. On one of the rocks Adam had scratched a picture, showing the six Earth scientists as large, solid creatures. The natives, in comparison, were small and barely more than stick figures. One figure, one of the Earth people, had been filled in, scratched in parallel rows of markings to indicate his color. This was obviously Leigh. In one hand he held several wavy lines—fire. At his feet were dead creatures, monkeys, deer, doglike animals. This was the food he had taught the natives to hunt. His other hand reached out to a figure like the fertility symbol someone had carved a few days before.

"It's very good," said Leigh, at a loss to know what to make of it.

"About forty thousand years too soon, also," said Engerev. "I wish Nkeida were here. She'd know, for sure."

"Screw her," said Leigh angrily.

"She could be lying dead not twenty yards from here," said Engerev. "Don't you think we could at least go up in the shuttle and cruise a bit, looking for her?"

"Black mother of lies does not die," said Adam.

"I wish I had your confidence," said Engerev.

118

"Screw her," said Leigh. He spat.

"Why?" said Engerev, laughing. "Because you couldn't?"

Leigh only spat again.

"Dr. Nkeida was the only single person on this crew most able to tell us what is happening here," said Engerev. "Personal difficulties aside for the moment—"

"Don't count on it," said Leigh, looking at Paula across the plain.

"—I think that either we should make some attempt to find and rescue her, or call off the mission altogether, before we spoil these people any further."

"I don't know if you've noticed," said Leigh casually, "but we haven't given them anything since the fire and the weapons. They have developed everything else on their own. What took our own ancestors hundreds of thousands of years to accomplish, these people have telescoped into days."

"The woman called Gretchen invented a device today," said Adam.

"Don't tell me," said Engerev, passing a weary hand over his eyes. "The internal combusion engine."

Adam looked puzzled. "A needle, Captain Giacomo called it. Now, we don't have to tie these skins on our bodies. Gretchen used some plaited grass and sewed a suit for herself. That can make the huts more permanent, too."

Engerev and Leigh spent some time arguing the proper thing to do, but the argument was mostly useless. As long as the combinations of the shuttle's locks were Leigh's secret, he had all the power. He could strand them all on the face of Jennings's World, while he alone returned to the ship in orbit, and then to Earth. So, after all, Engerev had to stop his argument. Judy Swan Nkeida would have to live or die on her own. "What about those people you saved on Mars?" asked Engerev.

"Figure it out," said Leigh.

"One of them was a man," said Engerev.

"He doesn't want to talk about it, and neither do I. It robs the whole episode of the heroic veneer the press gave it. I like the idea of me urging these wretches on across the filthy face of Mars. I like it a lot better than the picture of a depraved menage crawling through the red dust."

"And if Nkeida had found you more to her liking?"

"She'd be here now, happily taking notes."

"Did you kill her?" asked Engerev.

"Don't be foolish. I just had Paula tell her of another group of natives who live in a kind of oasis about ten miles from here. She got herself fixed up with allergy shots and took off. She'll be back. So now, this way, she can have her cake and eat it, too. She can study a group of unspoiled savages. What a boring way to spend a year."

CHAPTER 8

Judy Swan Nkeida was tired and hungry when she finally found the community of the "other people." These savages were in the same state as the first group had been when the research team discovered it. They did not have fire. They ate only the vegetable matter nearby. They did not seem to have any kind of family or clan ties. Nkeida was almost deliriously happy.

She put down three tape machines around the edge of the community, being especially careful not to be seen. She spoke into her field recorder often, making notes to herself, reporting information to the master computer aboard the *Unexpected Guest*. "I can't afford to be spotted," she said at one point early in her investigation. "There have been no signs of any blacks among these people. I would be too strange a phenomenon for them." She ignored the kind of phenomenon Cdr. Paul Leigh had become for the first tribe. Dr. Nkeida had no desire to be worshipped.

The tape machines recorded everything that happened for several days. This was mostly repetitious rounds of eating and mating. Food-gathering consumed the greatest part of the time; digging roots and tubers and gathering berries and nuts went on in an individual fashion, without any community thought at all. If a member was too old or too sick to gather his own food, he did not eat that day. "Survival of the fittest," sighed Nkeida into her recorder. "How I hate that. Even survival of the strongest might be better, because the strongest might take a liking to one of the weaker members, and protect the weak. But there's no arguing around survival of the fittest. I have never felt either strong or fit."

In the brush around Nkeida's own campsite, about a mile away from the community she called "Specimen B," animals moved with quick, rushing sounds. She was frightened, but she had one of the handguns with her. There had not been a sign of a dangerous carnivore at either site, but that did not mean that there were none. It just meant that they left no signs.

Nkeida's rations were running out, and she realized that she would have to live off the land for possibly many months. She followed the sounds of the animals and was led to a stream, possibly the same stream that had been near their original landing point. And the food of the savages would do for her, too; she could do without cooking it, and she could live without meat.

Weeks went by, weeks filled with an awful boredom and loneliness. Many times Nkeida almost gave in and returned to "Specimen A," but the memory of Cdr. Leigh prevented her. She would suffer if she had to, but she would not return a failure. She would save the mission from itself. She would be hailed as a scientific hero when they returned. Already, the computer was crammed with the dull facts of life about these brutes. No incest taboos, no ideas of personal or community hygiene, no ambition, no desire to communicate. These people were virtual ciphers. Animals in zoos had more to offer.

Dr. Nkeida caught herself. She had begun making value judgments, the kind of thing that would taint her findings. She decided that perhaps a few days of vacation, a relaxation of her vigilance, might restore a freshness to her viewpoint. She decided to explore the territory farther on.

In all the weeks that the research team had been on Jennings's World, the climate had not changed. It seemed that the seasons differed only very slightly. Perhaps the polar tilt of the planet was much less than Earth's. Whatever the reason, the people who inhabited the planet did not see any reason to put aside food for the winter. Even those uneducated brutes would have learned the cycle of

122

the seasons; if a harsh winter were approaching, they would show some sign of anxiety.

Logic told her to follow the course of the stream. It wound around lazily through the tall grass; Nkeida walked in the shallow water when she could, to avoid having to brush the irritating grass away from her face. Her allergy to the stuff had never abated, but Ajez's shots had helped. Several miles downstream, she encountered "Specimen C." She was amazed to find that this group of natives, unlike the other two, had come a long way toward civilization on its own. The people lived in huts, much like those Leigh had taught the people of "Specimen A" to use. The huts were spaced rather farther apart, and among them were what were obviously tilled fields. There was a large central corral, and some milk-giving animals were kept there. The animals did not seem to be entirely domesticated. They kicked and butted anyone who came near; milk had to be taken from them by teams of people.

Nkeida was excited. She wondered about the differences in the ways of life among the three specimens. She put down her recorders outside "Specimen C" and waited. She did not have to wait long for an explanation. About an hour after she arrived, she heard one of the people say, in English, "Do you want to try to milk that deer again, or should we just cut her up for dinner?"

That answered Nkeida's questions. Contamination. She picked up her recorders, made a hasty note to herself in her field machine, and began the walk back to "Specimen B." The day was warm, and the cool water of the stream felt good. While she walked, she tried to imagine how "Specimen C" could have been contaminated already. Cdr. Leigh would never have left "A" voluntarily; he was a god. Perhaps that status would change when it was discovered that he could not father a child on Paula—even if that were true. More likely, though, the people would blame Paula. She might even be put to death or exiled.

Engerev? No. He was staying around to put whatever check he could on Leigh's power. Engerev had ambition of his own, but not enough to leave the community and start his own nation.

Bernacek? Never. Ajez? Never.

123

That left the white woman, Carolyn Giacomo. And the idea fitted. Giacomo wanted another equal community so that there might be a chance for conflict. Conflict was what Giacomo lived for.

A new idea occurred to Nkeida. She slowly developed the thought that an interesting study might be made of the different ways the specimens turned out, depending on whose personality guided them. That kind of study would have to be kept secret from the other members of the research team, but that wouldn't be difficult, either; they paid her little enough attention. And "Specimen B" would be the control group. She would keep it uncontaminated as long as possible.

Judy Swan Nkeida slept on the banks of the stream that night, uneasily, afraid. The next morning she awoke and rubbed her stiff muscles. She couldn't turn her head to the right without pain. But she got up and finished the journey back to "Specimen B." She crept up on the edge of the community. She stopped and stared. Her control group was building huts, putting up a corral, planting small gardens. "All right," she cried," walking into the center of the village, "who did it? Who spoiled these people?"

"We just shared with them," said a native. Nkeida thought she recognized the man as a resident of Specimen A."

"Did one of our group come here with you?" asked Nkeida.

"No," said the man, whose name Nkeida remembered was Larry.

Nkeida was furious, but helpless. She couldn't very well deny progress to a race of humans because they would be more interesting otherwise. Now every idea she had had was ruined, even the study of specimen as reflection of founding personality. Perhaps "Specimen C" had not been started by Giacomo, after all. Everything was broken, again. Everything that she had worked to build, to save, to salvage, everything was ruined. She was a failure again.

"Are you hungry, black mother of lies?" asked Larry.

Nkeida looked up, her eyes flashing with anger. "Who told you to call me that?"

"No one told us," said Larry. "We understood it ourselves. You are the exact opposite of the great god Leigh. You pretend to be like him, with the blackness of your skin. But there is only one great god. There can be only one. So you must lie. You must be the great black mother of lies."

"And the others? The white woman? The men?"

"They are Leigh's slaves. You proved that you were the mother of lies by leaving our village. You are not Leigh's slave."

"That's very, very true," said Nkeida.

"You must be almost his equal, but evil."

Suddenly Nkeida felt very giddy and lightheaded. She had worked through her childhood, she had fought, she had struggled, she had gotten onto this research team, had been asleep for four years, landed on another world, just to be called the essence of evil. It was crazy. It was funny. Nkeida started to laugh.

Larry turned to the people of "Specimen B." "She is mad," he said. "But she is very clever. Never, never listen to anything she says. She is the black mother of lies. She can convince you that day is night, that hunger is fullness, that an ancient love is hatred. When you go forth from here, when you meet others of our brothers and sisters, tell them what I have told you. Tell them of living in huts and how to build them. Tell them of growing food and never searching for good places to eat again. Tell them of taming animals for milk and meat. Give them fire and stone weapons. Tell them first of the great god Leigh. Tell them again of the great god Leigh. And warn them about the black mother of lies."

"How many villages like this are there?" asked Nkeida.

Larry stood silently for a moment. "There are many," he said at last. "Your work will be hard."

"I'm going home," she said. "Want to come with me?"

Larry only shuddered. Nkeida smiled.

"They've moved into the Neolithic," said Nkeida to Ajez, when she had returned to "Specimen A."

"And we've watched them. We've seen them do it," said the medical officer.

"That's a lot of territory to make up in a few weeks."

"And we haven't given them a thing," said Ajez, shaking his head. "Nothing but the fire and the weapons. Stone weapons, at that. Clubs, maybe. And they've developed so fast."

"Where's Giacomo?" asked Nkeida.

"Oh," said Ajez, "she got her wish. She talked about half of the people here into going off with her to found a new village. She said the hunting near here would run out soon. Leigh gave her two handguns and a rifle. We'll hear from her soon, no doubt."

"That's awful," said Nkeida.

"That's progress," said Ajez with a wry smile.

"Who invented agriculture?" asked Nkeida. "I wish I'd seen that."

"Some woman named Sharon, I think," said Ajez. "It was after Giacomo went away with her half of the village. They tore down the empty huts, and the space became fields. It was just one of those sudden things. The same for domesticating these animals. They don't even have names for them yet. But Giacomo's arguments got them to thinking. They decided to have the food here, rather than have to go out for it every day."

"I'm surprised no one's thought to dig a canal from the stream," said Nkeida.

"They're out doing that today."

"Terrific." The woman and the man stood for a while, silently gazing at the laboring villagers. Every person seemed to have a job to do. "Do you know," said Nkeida, "that there are villages just like this that we haven't even had contact with?"

"So I've heard. Lots of them." Ajez chewed his lip for a moment. "God, what have we done?"

"I told you so, I told you so, I told you so," said Nkeida, shaking her head.

"Yeah, but you're the black mother of lies."

"Yeah, and you're the brown father of toads, too." Ajez didn't laugh. "I'm sorry, Sanchito."

"All right. I was just thinking about Leigh. About when it's time to go home again. What will he do then?"

"Why don't you ask him now, while he's still partially

sane?" said Nkeida. "We ought to be able to get some kind of bargain out of him."

"Engerev's already tried that. Leigh won't say a word."

"We may be in trouble."

Ajez looked at the woman. "For the black mother of lies, you sure hit the nail on the head."

"I have my finger on the pulse of the problem," she said. "I hope you don't think I've usurped your role."

"No," said Ajez. "Fortunately, there hasn't even been a case of strep throat. We're healthy, and they're healthy, and I get to sleep late every morning."

"Well, thank God for that," said Nkeida, looking disgusted. "At least we have our health. The people back on Earth will be gratified."

"The people back on Earth may never know."

"Wouldn't that be too bad? Wouldn't that be a major disappointment to whoever is waiting for word? They send us off and then sit by their radios for ten years, waiting, waiting, candles burning in the living room windows—"

"Judy."

"I'm sorry," said Nkeida. "I'm still reacting to the failure of our mission. This wasn't what we were sent out here for. Leigh had experience, they said. They didn't look too closely at what kind of experience. His mental profile fitted best, they said, but how do we know? How do we know those profiles were healthy? Maybe they selected exactly the wrong people for every job on this mission. Surely, there must have been a social anthropologist somewhere better qualified than me."

"It's too late for any of that," said Ajez.

Their conversation was interrupted by the arrival of Engerev, Benarcek, and Leigh. They were all glad to see Dr. Nkeida again.

"We thought you might just have wandered off," said Benarcek.

"That's what I did," said Nkeida.

"But you're back safe," said Leigh. "That's the important thing."

"Is your black mother of lies so important?" she asked.

"Ha-ha," said Leigh, without much humor. "I'm glad

127

you can take that without offense." Nkeida didn't answer.

There were many villages. There were dozens of them, all linked by the spreading of knowledge from "Specimen A." Each village, once it had caught up to the others, felt compelled to go out and teach the small communities of savages they knew lived nearby. These communities merged into towns. Families assumed identities. Property was no longer communal, because of the need to keep ownership straight, lines of descent were invented; inheritance was along the mother's side, as everyone tended to be polygamous. Incest taboos arose; chiefly out of a desire to keep the inheritance matter as simple as possible. What was the proper line of descent if you were your own father or mother, son or daughter?

The villages and towns began to differentiate among themselves. After a short while some places became noted for the superiority of one product or another. Trade sprang up, as a village that produced poor stone axes sent to another village for them, using food or another product as the medium of exchange.

As commerce among the villages grew, transportation became important, as well. Paths through the high grasses were trampled, leading from "Specimen A," which, because of Leigh's residency, seemed to be the capital of the small towns, to other nearby villages. These trampled routes were made more passable by cutting the grasses back with sharp stone axes. Towns worked together on these projects, because benefits to everyone were obvious. When the grass had been cleared away, a runner could reach the next town in a few hours without discomfort, without having to brush the grass away, thus allowing him to carry things in his arms.

Leigh instituted certain practices, because he didn't want to start a kind of primitive Communism. Everyone took a share of food, whether he worked or not. So Leigh made those who weren't engaged in any worthwhile pursuits, making any useful products for trade, or working in the fields, volunteer for roadwork. Stones and boulders were dug out of the cleared paths and tossed aside. Holes were filled in. The grasses, which grew back quickly, were trimmed away every week. This way, the idle of each community were put to useful labor. The food was no longer doled out in equal and impartial lots. Workers received payment in food. The primitive artisans were paid in food or articles that could be traded for food. Soon, wooden or bone beads came to represent the articles themselves; currency was invented, so that people didn't actually have to carry pots or axes or animals from place to place, just to trade for food. These beads were commonly accepted at a certain set rate, a rate established by Leigh.

One day, a young man who made clay pots decided to take a selection of his handicraft to a nearby village that had no one to compete with his pots. He had a problem, though, of transporting a large number of pots. He put them on a skin and tried dragging it behind him, but it soon became clear that by the time he arrived at the next village the pots would all be broken. He appealed to Leigh, and the great god Leigh passed his first miracle since he had shown the savages how to build huts. He invented the wheel for them, and in a short while the young potter had a cart. He pulled it himself; it was a while before anyone thought of harnessing a tamed deer or cow to use as a draft animal.

Every day, every week brought refinements in their way of life. No one knew where the first metal-shod spears came from. It was evidently some village a good distance from "Specimen A" because they had been traded time and again, and their owners' marks were carved up and down the shafts. But the superiority of the metal-tipped spears over the bone and wood spears was evident. They became the most sought-after commodity in the society. The village that produced them became rich, until other towns learned the secret and began making their own metal products. So, from the new Stone Age, the savages, the natives, the aborigines, the *people* moved into the Bronze Age, five thousand years behind their Earthly teachers.

Carts were traveling back and forth, and the villages that through luck were located on the intersections of the crude roads became marketplaces. "Specimen A" never lost its dominance, but other towns grew up strong and powerful in their own rights, for different reasons.

One day, on a journey to a village three days' ride from "Specimen A," Sanchito Ajez saw something on the road ahead. When he got closer, he saw that a battle had been fought and the area was littered with corpses. He judged that the battle had occurred only a day before, from the state of the dead bodies. He had a terrible moment when he recognized Carolyn Giacomo as one of the dead. She was pinned to the ground with one of the new metal-tipped spears through her torso, just below her breastbone. Near one hand was a handgun. Ajez checked it; it was empty of its charge. He shook his head. "There's a lot to be said for a weapon that doesn't need reloading," he murmured. He put Giacomo's corpse in the back of his cart and turned around, to take her back to "Specimen A" for burial.

When Ajez brought Giacomo's corpse up to Leigh's new, larger hut, Dr. Justin Benarcek saw what had happened. For a moment he became hysterical. "We weren't supposed to die here," he shouted. "We weren't supposed to *die* here!" He held his head, shading his eyes with his fingers. He tried to turn away, but he couldn't. Leigh came out to see what was causing the excitement.

"Oh, Lord," said Leigh, when he saw the woman's body. "I hope she likes it in Valhalla."

"She will, until you get there," said Nkeida.

"They got another place all marked out for me," said Leigh, with his evil grin.

"Yeah," said Nkeida, who was the first to think of closing Giacomo's eyes.

"I'm sorry this had to spoil what would have been a lovely day," said Leigh. "Our stonecutters are beginning work today on the first stone building. A palace for me and Paula and Suzy and Tammy. And someone, I forget who, was showing me the first few stanzas of a poetic work, some epic about me or something."

"All these things," said Benarcek.

"I'd date us about the beginning of the Christian era,

now," said Dr. Judy Swan Nkeida, as she walked away. No one ever saw her again.

"We weren't supposed to *die* here," murmured Benarcek.

PART FIVE

2029

CHAPTER 9

During the next several years, the face of Jennings's World changed. When the research team had landed in 2021, the planet had been inhabited by the most primitive of savages. According to the computer aboard the dormant *Unexpected Guest*, it was only eight years later. But judging from the way the world had progressed, an innocent observer might have supposed centuries had gone by. In a subjective sense, they had. In those eight years the people of Jennings's World had made up the two-thousand-year gap in technology and social structure that separated them from their visitors. The men from Earth watched, awed, as discovery after discovery, invention after invention were made, brought forth, nonchalantly discussed. Almost every individual in the community contributed, and there was a minimum of trial-and-error work—either that, or the first trials were generally correct.

Years had passed since the time when the crew of the space vehicle was due to return, first to the shuttle, then to the mother ship in orbit. The four remaining members of the crew ought to have placed themselves back in suspended animation for the long voyage home. But when the prescribed time came, Benarcek, Engerev, and Ajez realized that Cdr. Leigh would not permit them to go without him, and he was not yet ready to leave. He had too much to keep himself occupied with on Jennings's World, and nothing but a tainted reputation back on Earth.

And Leigh was occupied. There had been no dark ages on Jennings's World, no wasted centuries of fear and ignorance. It had been a constant, never slowing flowering of learning. It was an amazing thing to watch, and it was even more incredible to take part. Cdr. Paul Drayden Leigh was taking part. Despite the scientific revolution that went on around him every day, he was still the great god Leigh. "Specimen A" grew from a collection of huts to a small town, then to a city, as more and more of the planet's former savages came to live and work near their ruler. The city was called Sun, and its inhabitants numbered twenty-five thousand.

It was unlikely that any group of still-savage people remained on the world. The missionary zeal with which the indoctrinated people sought out the uninformed, produced the startling changes that Leigh watched with so much satisfaction. There were other cities, as well, and they were linked by broad, paved highways. Buildings of ten and twenty stories were commonplace. Knowledge was recorded in books, and the development of communications media enabled everyone in every city to have access to new ideas.

Leigh emptied the contents of the space shuttle for the use of his subjects. He provided them with computers and other technical apparatus that further expanded their knowledge. By the end of the eighth year, the people of Jennings's World had matched the level of civilization of Cdr. Leigh's own Earth, in all but some superficial ways. The buildings were not as tall as the skyscrapers on Earth, but that was because the population was less dense. There had been fewer advances made in the arts, but that was because eight years did not provide adequate time to develop aesthetic movements. The popular literary form was the epic; the popular artistic format was the portrait. These pleased Leigh, and so they had his official sanction.

One afternoon, one of the former primitives brought Cdr. Leigh a new epic, celebrating Leigh's special qualities, his generosity, his leadership abilities, and his sexual prowess. The epic was some five hundred pages long, written in the iambic pentameter that Leigh favored. The great black god was especially pleased by the work and ordered that it be printed immediately and distributed throughout the world, in time for the annual celebration of the disappearance of Judy Swan Nkeida, who had never been found. Nkeida had been made into a kind of saint by Leigh, who had forgotten in his egotistical way the manner in which Nkeida had loathed him. It never occurred to Leigh that an epic celebrating her might be more appropriate.

The books were finished in two weeks. Sanchito Ajez, Justin Benarcek, and Alexei Engerev were given copies from the first ten off the presses, autographed by Cdr. Paul Drayden Leigh rather than the author; the three scientists accepted the books with mixed feelings.

"What does this mean?" asked Engerev.

"I don't know," said Ajez.

"It means that somewhere we went wrong," said Benarcek.

"How about that," said Engerev cynically. "But it wasn't us that went wrong. It was Leigh and his fire tricks.'

Ajez chewed his lip. "Yeah," he said, "but he's a great god, and what are we? The bastards always get all the breaks. We don't get epics written about us. We're not even lesser gods. We're supposed to be Leigh's slaves or something, as I understand it."

"The mythos isn't very consistent," said Engerev.

Benarcek slammed the book closed. He had been reading a few pages while Ajez and Engerev talked. "Boy," he said, sighing, "this is really terrible. This is about the worst poetry I've ever read. It makes Elizabeth Dawson Douglas look like Homer."

"Who is Elizabeth Dawson Douglas?" asked Ajez.

"I think they melted her down toward the end of the twentieth century," said Engerev.

At that moment, there was a knock on the door of the chamber, and Leigh entered, grinning and looking very pleased. "How do you like it?" he asked.

"We just got them," said Ajez. "We haven't had time to read them yet. Are we going to be tested on this material?" Leigh ignored the Mexican medical officer.

"You know," said Engerev, "when you gave them fire, I thought, well, maybe we had interfered with their culture. I had my doubts about the propriety of doing that, but I said to myself, 'What could happen? What could go wrong? So they have fire. Maybe they'll invent the spear. In a couple of thousand years they'll have the arrow. So what?' I wasn't set for something like this."

"You mean the epic?" asked Leigh, looking pleased again.

"No," said Engerev.

"This guy really makes me look good," said Leigh. "Maybe I'll appoint him poet laureate or something like that."

"I think the best thing would be shock therapy," said Ajez.

"There's a scene toward the middle where I screw about five hundred women in order to escape from a tyrant," said Leigh.

"I wish it were that easy," murmured Engerev.

"Anyway," said Leigh, "it's a good book, full of adventure and a lot of clever little bits. I think it'll sell. There haven't been many good epics in the last month or so. I wonder why that is."

"Religious repression," said Ajez.

This time, Leigh did not ignore Ajez. "All right," he said, "that's enough. I was going to try to be nice to you guys because, after all, we're from the same place and we're partners in this thing."

"I'm glad that occurs to you every now and then," said Engerev. "I was beginning to think you were born here. Or in space somewhere, and then you created this world. Great god Leigh."

"Yes," said Leigh. "Great god. Well, you know the part you're supposed to play?"

"Your slaves," said Benarcek.

"Right," said Leigh. "Well, I've never made you have to act that out, but from now on things will be a little more realistic."

"I should have kept my mouth shut about that," said Engerev.

"These people look up to me as their god and their leader," said Leigh. "I'm special. But that doesn't mean that they don't have their own local leaders. It's a matter of practicality. The cities have their lords, and the states have their sovereigns, and the continents have their overlords. Well, these people have been after me for some time to keep you in line, because it hurts their authority, and mine, too, to have you acting so free and unslave-like."

"Do you want us to go around with our heads bowed?" asked Benarcek.

"We could sit out on our cabin steps and play banjos and sing spirituals," said Ajez.

"Shut up," said Leigh. "Actually, it won't be so bad. It's just kind of a token thing that I suggested to the overlords, and they agreed. You'll all be given apartments, luxuriously furnished, with everything you could possibly want. I mean it. Food or women or anything. But you can't leave the apartments."

There was a moment of silence. "What?" said Benarcek.

"We're prisoners?" said Ajez.

"I wouldn't think of it like that," said Leigh.

"No," said Engerev, "you wouldn't. But we would."

"Too bad," said Leigh, "because there's no way to change anything. You don't have anything to say about the matter."

"Look," said Engerev angrily, "we came from Earth. Remember? It wasn't so long ago. We were all living on Earth, rather comfortably, all members of the same species, all each other's keepers. You can't suddenly declare yourself our master like this."

"It wasn't so sudden," said Leigh. "And while we may have been species-mates, we were and are of different races. You may notice the different pigmentations of our skins. That is what sets us apart. That is what makes me the great god Leigh."

"Is that what it was?" asked Ajez. "Then what about Nkeida?"

"What about her?" asked Leigh.

"The black mother of lies," said Engerev. "Remember that?"

"No," said Leigh, "not exactly."

"Well, it's in your epic," said Benarcek.

"Your apartments will be ready soon," said Leigh. "Ring if you want anything. Until we have your places fixed up, you'll have to stay here. I'll check with you in a while." And with that, Leigh turned and left, paying no attention to the consternation he had caused among his shipmates.

In a few days, they were moved to their new apartments. As Leigh had said, they were beautifully furnished with all the luxury items that anyone might want. But Ajez, Benarcek, and Engerev looked on their interconnecting rooms as cells, and that's what they were.

Outside, the world of the former savages was going through its accelerating upheaval. Things had not slowed, and in a matter of days many things had happened to change the political and social order again. The institution of production lines and the adoption of interchangeable parts had the same revolutionary effect on Jennings's World that it had had on Earth. Many workers were thrown out of jobs, and the economy of the planet was shaken. Leigh started welfare programs, and he was praised for the idea. It had not yet occurred to any of his subjects. Leigh smiled and accepted the adulation modestly, or, rather, what he believed to be modestly.

An adviser spoke to him shortly thereafter with a scheme to spur the economy and increase productivity. "Planned obsolescence," said the man.

"An interesting term," said Leigh.

"I made it up myself," said the adviser. "It's rather self-explanatory. We make these products to fall apart after so long, so that the consumer has to purchase new things to replace them."

"Do it," said Leigh, and in a few hours it was done. A few days later, thanks to some poor speculation and uninformed economic forecasting, Leigh was faced with a planetwide depression. The number of unemployed grew, and inflation was rampant. Leigh asked for cooperation from everyone, pleaded with the larger corporations to forgo their private interests for the moment for the benefit of the general welfare, and within thirty-six hours the depression had ended. All over Jennings's World, poets began new epics in honor of the great god Leigh. Ajez, Benarcek, and Engerev watched the developments on television and ate the best food available. Ajez was visited by dutiful young women almost every night, Benarcek less often, and Engerev never. The Russian could not rid himself of guilty thoughts about his wife, Ireyn, and his children.

The months passed, and the growth on Jennings's World did not slow. Judy Swan Nkeida, the ethnographer, had estimated that the average life span of the primitives had been between twenty-eight and thirty-four years. It was likely that never before had anyone on that harsh world existed more than four decades. Now, because of the radical improvement in living conditions, food production, and medical care, it was impossible to estimate what the average life span might be. And the credit, as always, went to the great god Leigh.

But things were changing in that area, too. The local leaders and the overlords of the continents were feeling the attraction of power. And it was true that to gain more power, one had to deprive someone else. The only person to deprive was Cdr. Leigh; after a time, after the promptings of ambition, several men decided that was not so evil a thing.

There were six of them, the overlords of the continents of Jennings's World. They called themselves Stan, Tom, Chuck, Ed, Nelson, and Denny. They met in frequent conferences to discuss their mutual plans; these meetings were never disclosed to Leigh, who might have seen in them a threat to his own authority. The overlords made decisions which would affect the future, not only for themselves personally, but for every one of the growing masses of people on the planet. And each decision was backed by a reasonable-sounding rationalization, which the overlords argued over until they convinced themselves that even Leigh, himself, would agree. But not one of them ever suggested that they ask the great god for his opinion.

"This planet on which we live," said Stan, the overlord of Continent 3, "is apparently unfit for our growing needs. We lack many of the raw materials needed for the increased production the great god Leigh has blessed us with. He has taught us about metals that we have not been able to find in the crust of our world. He has created in us a longing for things that our home planet cannot

141

provide. This can lead only to frustration, unhappiness, social unrest, and even civil disorder."

One of the other overlords rose to his feet and looked around the table at his fellows. This was Nelson, the overlord of Continent 6, and he was a pompous bureaucrat, because one day he had overheard the great god Leigh describing that kind of leader to one of Leigh's advisers. Nelson, although he was not a pompous person by nature, felt that anything that was part of Leigh's vast store of knowledge deserved its representation on Jennings's World. So he volunteered to be the pompous bureaucrat among them. In private, however, and among the closed company of his fellow overlords, he dropped that pose gratefully. "I agree," he said, nodding toward Stan. "Our technology and our capabilities grow with each passing day, and they must be fed. Our workers can barely keep up. The unemployed have been put to work exploiting our natural resources and searching for new deposits of the fuels and minerals we need. But if these deposits do not exist, then we will be faced with a slowing down of progress, and then those evil situations Stan outlined. We owe it to our world and our constituents to see that this does not happen. I, for one, do not relish the idea of relating to my people the reasons that they will have to accept a cutback in their standard of living. Soon we will slide backward, back toward the uncivilized barbarism from which the great god Leigh rescued us. That, beyond all else, would be blasphemy, in its own way. Yes, that's true. More than to ourselves and our people, we owe it to the great god Leigh to see to it that the enrichment of our lives never suffers suspension because of a mere lack of physical matter." Nelson sat down quickly, embarrassed by the length and pomposity of his speech.

Tom, the overlord of Continent 1, spoke up without standing. He talked in a slow, thoughtful manner, and he commanded the attention and respect of all who heard him. "Let us puzzle this out together," he said. "What is the name of our home planet? Jennings's World. And who or what is Jennings?"

"The great god Leigh explained to us that Jennings was a great man from Leigh's own home," said Nelson.

"Exactly," said Tom. "Then what does that suggest to you? I offer the following. In the great god's own words, Jennings was 'a great man.' Not a god. A man. Like you or me. Why is this plane not called Leigh?"

"I have never been able to understand that myself," said Ed, the overlord of Continent 5.

"Also in the great god's own words," said Tom, "this Jennings was from 'Leigh's own home.' Do gods have homes, and do they share them with men?"

"Leigh is doing that here," said Stan. "With us."

"Yes," said Tom slowly. "But from the great god's talks, it has sounded to me as though there were a world where Leigh and his slaves came from. This world is a planet, just as Jennings's World is a planet. The only difference was that its inhabitants were our intellectual superiors. But this may no longer be true. The great god has said this himself, often."

"That is right," said Ed. "And this home of the great god is called Earth."

"Quite right," said Tom. "It is my opinion that Earth is merely another world which was rescued from savagery by the great god Leigh. He arrived there with his slaves Benarcek, Ajez, and Engerev, along with the black mother of lies, and did for the brutes he found there precisely what he did for us."

"That sounds very reasonable," said Chuck, the overlord of Continent 2.

"Fine," said Tom. "If we are all agreed on that, then, I believe that it follows logically that the great god Leigh left Earth for reasons of his own."

"You could say that he abandoned Earth," said Stan.

"And chose our planet instead," said Tom. "In that case, there is no reason to think that Earth has any special importance to him. There is every encouragement to believe that Earth has been left on its own, with the great god's sanction withdrawn and bestowed instead on us."

"And evidently Earth has the very resources we so badly require," said Nelson.

There was a moment of quiet, as the overlords considered how to phrase what they were all thinking.

"Earth has been prepared for us," said Denny, the overlord of Continent 4.

"Earth has been delivered into our keeping," said Tom, "and was developed chiefly to provide for us in our moment of need."

"That is a comforting thought," said Chuck.

"The great god Leigh has always provided for us, and given us comfort," said Tom. "Now he has done so again, and it is up to us to take this opportunity to save our world."

Nelson spoke up. "As I said before, it would be blasphemous not to. That becomes clearer and clearer."

"Well, then," said Tom softly, "let's do it."

Three hours later, Chuck, the overlord of Continent 2, was back in his capital city, which was called Rain. A few minutes after his plane landed, he was speaking by telephone to several of his chief advisers. "Listen," he said to them as they listened in their various offices, "we have to develop space travel."

"We're working on it, I think," said one of the advisers. "At least, there were some scientists over in Continent 1 who were trying to get that study moving. That's one of the areas in which we haven't quite matched the great god Leigh's reports of Earth."

"We have the theoretical knowledge, I think," said another adviser.

"Check on it," said Chuck.

"Right," said the adviser, who picked up another phone and called one of his own advisers.

"And not only space travel," said Chuck, "but interstellar travel. I've just returned from very important high-level conferences, and it was generally agreed that interstellar commerce is our best hope to sustain our cherished ideals."

"Our accelerating rate of progress should be producing interstellar travel soon," said a third adviser. "We have a good deal of confidence in that."

Chuck sighed; he hated having to deal with these stupid men. "I understand that," he said patiently. "But I'm talking about right now. The normal scarcity of materials and production time-lag would slow the projects down too much. I'm speaking of having the whole thing finished by the end of the year."

"We'll see what we can do," said an adviser.

"See what you can do," said Chuck. He cut the connection on his phone.

On Continent 4, in the city of Wind, Denny held a conference of his own advisers the next morning. He had received a detailed report from Chuck concerning the status of the various projects working toward the development of interstellar space travel. Now he was trying to get his subordinates to comprehend his instructions. He was frustrated at how difficult it was to deal with even his best aides. Even these carefully chosen men often had trouble taking his desires and finding efficient ways of fulfilling them.

"What we are going to do," said Denny, "is set up a panel that will graph our progress to date, use the computers to extrapolate our progress in the near future, and draw up a timetable for the completion of this thing. I want an hour-by hour breakdown including all technical, engineering, chemical, and medical problems that need to be solved, and the estimated time of their solution. That's not too difficult to understand, is it?"

"No, sir," said one of he advisers.

"Good," said Denny. "Then get going on it. I want this panel to come up with the improvements first, instead of working out the bugs in the systems. I want no delays. I want it all now."

"That production time-lag is a tough thing to avoid," said one of the advisers. "No matter how much the guys in the shops know about what they have to do, they still have to do it, and that takes a certain amount of time."

"The panel will make that the minimum amount of time," said Denny.

"Right," said the adviser, chastened.

"There was a negative report," said another adviser timidly. "It predicted that the rate of progress as drawn on a graph will be a curve drastically flattened, in comparison to the rapidly rising curve of the previous few years. The report said that the possibility exists that, having about equalled the level of technology of Earth, at the time when the great god Leigh left that world we could expect that our own advancement would stall."

145

"Who did this report?" asked Denny, yawning.

"Some odd religious group," said the adviser.

Denny only shrugged. Some of the other advisers laughed quietly.

The preparations were completed and the interstellar research went on, partially in secret, because the overlords had decided that the great god Leigh might not understand their motives until they could present the matter to him in a humble manner. It was very difficult for the overlords to discuss their schemes with humility; they had all their otherwise unemployed advisers working on that. Meanwhile, the interstellar project proceeded, disguised by code names. The overlords were Group One. The guiding panel of statisticians and future-planners was Group Two.

In the city of Sun, not far from the great god Leigh's own splendid palace, Group Two met for its final, conclusive session. Graphs were studied by the hour and by the hundreds of pages. All the resources of the planet, material and social, were defined in intersecting lines or looping curves on those graphs. They were necessarily very complex, and their interrelationships escaped all but the closest study. Finally, though, Group Two made its judgments and wrote up a summary for Group One. All the aspects were good and the outlook was positive. The great god Leigh would be flattered.

Tom, the overlord of Continent 1, received his copy of the summary an hour later. He read it quickly, with a great deal of concealed excitement. It would be his duty to take the report and discuss the matter with Leigh. It was a meeting that the overlord was not happy about, but armed with Group Two's estimates and predictions, he felt more confident.

"So you want to go to Earth," said Cdr. Leigh to the overlord.

"Yes, sir," said Tom. "We think that it is the best thing for us, and the most respectful thing we could do for you."

"I agree, I agree," said Leigh, laughing softly to himself while he stroked a small doglike animal that sat in his lap.

"I'm very happy to hear that," said Tom, knowing from

the report of Group Two that Leigh would say precisely those words. "We were somewhat worried that you might not understand."

"No need for concern, no need at all. In fact, I intend to accompany your first fleet, as commander-in-chief."

Tom sat, struck silent by the great god's pronouncement. This was something that Group Two had not foreseen at all. The overlord did not know exactly how to proceed, now that the meeting had moved away from its predicted course. "Would that be wise, sir?" asked Tom, trying to keep his voice respectful. "I mean, what about Jennings's World? Our people need you here."

"You're doing a fine job, Tom. You and the overlords and your juniors. You're not planning to go in the first fleet, are you?"

"No," said Tom.

"Well, then," said Leigh, "I can go and leave you in charge. I want to see the looks on their faces. But I won't want to stay. I'll be back to take over for you in your old age."

"I'm relieved to hear that, sir," said Tom, wanting nothing more than to get out of the chamber, out of the palace, and back to his own office. Suddenly there were a number of phone calls that he had to make.

CHAPTER 10

Group Two took the information that the great god Leigh desired to accompany the first fleet; Group Two expressed no opinions, it only predicted the advances in science and the changes in the social environment. It was up to Group One to make opinions, and the overlords hesitated in this matter. It was always better to let the great god Leigh have his way.

On the day that the shuttle craft was to be loaded with the passengers for the large fleet which now orbited Jennings' World, Cdr. Paul Drayden Leigh awoke from a troubled night's sleep. He realized that he, alone, would be returning to Earth, out of the company of scientists who had been sent to study the planet of the star Wolf 359. But Leigh would not be unaccompanied. He would be taking with him many thousands of people, all of whom had been the most barbaric savages only a few years before. But primitive they were no longer, and the people of Earth would soon learn what happens to nosy neighbors.

Leigh was driven to the shuttle craft that had been fitted for his own private use. He had his own pilot and navigator, and his favorite women were aboard to make his flight comfortable. They would all be placed in suspended animation together, and they would all awaken in Earth orbit together. Then the fleet would discharge its passengers, the shuttle craft would land them on every continent on Earth, and Commander Paul Drayden Leigh would write an indelible page in the history of two worlds. The entire affair made him nervous with anticipation.

The flight in the shuttle craft was uneventful; only the sight through the ports of the great fleet lying motionless above the giant sphere of Jennings's World impressed Leigh. There were an even hundred ships, glittering in the blackness of space like massive constellations of stars. The ships were built along the lines of the *Unexpected Guest*, although they would take seventeen years to reach Earth. Leigh expected to spend only a few months at the most on his home world, and then he would return in triumph to Jennings's World, some thirty-five years from the moment of his departure. Tom and the other overlords would be dead or very old, and Leigh would still be young. It made no difference to Leigh that these ships were much slower than the *Unexpected Guest* had been; indeed, the greater time span involved suited his plans perfectly. He would return in time to regain his power and influence and make his mark on a whole new generation of subjects. He would crush the power of the overlords, which had been growing too great and would continue to do so in his absence. But he would always be the great god Leigh. He was not worried about the future. He was only finding it difficult to control his eagerness.

The shuttle docked with the orbiting ship to which it had been assigned. Leigh stood up and prepared to disembark; his entourage followed him, carrying the cases which contained his personal effects. As Leigh walked through the new, clean, odd-smelling corridors of the ship, he was struck by an irritating detail. Everyone else on the ship was either too sick to move or crippled in some way. All of these unfortunate people were attended by doctors and nurses, who also would be placed in suspended animation along with their charges. Leigh could understand that the overlords of Jennings's World might want to rid themselves of the sick and crippled, and place these nonproductive members of the society under the care of the people of Earth. When he thought about it, Leigh agreed that it was an imaginative step. But he was piqued that he should have been placed aboard the same ship carrying these people. He would have preferred to have ridden on one of the other ships, with the armed might of Jennings's World. It would not be so impressive for him to disembark on Earth from the hospital ship. Perhaps the overlords believed that he would get better care; Leigh felt they had made a mistake, but it was too late to change it now. There was a rigid timetable. Grumbling, Leigh allowed himself to be placed in his suspension niche. In a few moments, he was asleep. He would remain asleep for seventeen years. It would be that long before he learned that everyone on every ship in the fleet, except his own party and the crews, was sick or crippled. The thousands who had boarded the great fleet were all deemed useless to Jennings's World, and they would live out their lives at the expense of another planet. Leigh traveled with them, mistakenly believing he was falling through space with a mighty fleet of soldiers.

Except for Leigh's own handgun, in the entire hundred ships there was not a single weapon.

About a week before the fleet was due to depart, an emissary from Group One was let into the apartment of Sanchito Ajez. The Mexican medical officer was surprised that anyone would visit him at that time of day. He stood silently, sullenly, while he waited for the government official to state his business.

"Have you heard about the space venture?" asked the emissary.

"Yes," said Ajez bitterly. "I read about it in the newsfiche."

"Good. We'd like your cooperation."

"I doubt that you'll get it."

The emissary shrugged. "I understand your attitude," he said. "Nevertheless. The situation is that our planning board has suggested that your medical knowledge would be indispensable to our fleet's passengers. Our own medical technology is based on the chemistry and biology of Jennings's World. Perhaps our doctors will have some difficulty when they arrive on Earth. There may be drastic differences which we are unable to predict. Therefore, as the only medical expert from Earth on our world, we would like you to accompany the fleet."

"You want me to help subdue my own people?" asked Ajez.

"No," said the emissary impatiently. "We just want your medical knowledge. You don't have to do anything at all about subduing your own people. Forget about that."

"I can't," said the large Mexican man. "I wouldn't do anything at all to help your effort. That's very simple, isn't it? You can understand, can't you? If you can't, take it back to Tom. He'll figure it all out sooner or later."

"You are right," said the emissary. "It's very simple." He turned and left the apartment. Ajez stared after him for several seconds, then he spat toward the door. The captive slumped down in a comfortable chair and stared thoughtfully at a wall for many minutes.

An hour later, three men dressed in white lab coats came to Ajez's apartment. Without saying a word, they entered; two of the men held Ajez while the third gave him an injection. He never woke up again. He was taken to a biological laboratory, where a team of technicians probed his memories using drugs and electrical stimuli. Ajez's complete personality was recorded on miles of invisible film, so thin that it was impossible for a human being to see the film or touch it. The film, containing not only the objective facts that were lodged in Ajez's brain but also the complete subjective attitudes that surrounded them, was used to indoctrinate the scores of doctors who rode the space fleet to Earth. Each one of them carried a transcription of Sanchito Ajez locked in his own mind.

After the recording of his memories, Ajez was reduced to less than a living animal. The technicians routinely destroyed what remained, and Ajez's corpse was disposed of with the rest of the day's waste. But in each of the doctors' heads resided what was individual about Sanchito Ajez, and in that way he, too, returned to the planet of his birth.

One month after the departure of the fleet, Group Two had a meeting to discuss what had been learned and what had been forecast since the writing of their report to Group One. A new project was initiated. With Leigh gone, the need for secrecy was gone, as well.

151

The chairman of Group Two called the session to order and congratulated his fellows on the success of the completed assignment. But he warned them that the future held more difficult challenges. "What's happening out there?" he asked. The various delegates gave their reports in turn.

"The ion-exchange engines of the first fleet will get it to Earth in seventeen years," said the delegate from Continent 1. "According to our estimates, someone will develop a superior propulsion unit within the next seven weeks. This propulsion unit, whatever it may turn out to be, will cut the time needed to journey between Jennings's World and Earth to eight years. We are not certain yet whether this invention will come from the work being done in Continent 1 by the research team headed by David, or from the team in Continent 4, headed by Marsha. I think we'll have to wait the whole seven weeks, but it's possible that we'll get an important hint before then. In that case, we can pull the other team off the project and direct them into something else."

"Good, very good," said the chairman. "Continent 2."

The delegate from that continent stood up and cleared his throat. "My graphs indicate that with the burden of the hopelessly ill and crippled removed, the economy has been positively affected by a factor of two point seven on the Christine scale. We can use that increase by channeling it into the project directly, and by using the resources thus liberated to advertise and propagandize our plans further. The unemployment situation is virtually nonexistent. We have the backing of ninety-seven point six percent of the population. We can carry on now in the name of the great god Leigh, using his official sanction on anything at all we wish to do. Therefore, my corps of statisticians has forecast that the next stage of the project should accelerate even more than we had previously figured. You will see from Graph Eighty that the new estimate is some three and a half degrees faster than the old."

"Thank you," said the chairman. He called on the next speaker, and the news from Continent 3 was equally optimistic. When the session concluded, a report was made and distributed to the overlords. Everyone was very happy.

Seven weeks later, the David Drive was perfected. That was on a Tuesday. By the following Sunday there were a hundred ships in orbit around Jennings's World, outfitted with the new propulsion unit that would get the ships to Earth in eight years, some nine years before the previous fleet would arrive. During those days of construction, the world was sifted for the thousands of farmers, craftsmen, and laborers who would make up the passenger list. Computers on each continent gave out lists of names of the chosen, along with efficiency and compatibility ratings. A final selection was made by a staff of the overlords' advisers, the individuals involved were notified, and the huge crowd of emigrants was assembled and housed overnight. On Monday morning, shuttle craft were ready and waiting to take the thousands of men and women to the orbiting vehicles.

At their conference center, the overlords watched the procedure on television. They were all gratified that Group Two was doing its job so well. That made their own job simpler. They could just relax and be overlords which, under normal circumstances, was a very enjoyable and comfortable position to be in. A crisis was always a crisis, of course, but if you had everyone's cooperation, as the overlords did, it reduced anxiety for everyone concerned.

"Well," said Tom, taking a look at his watch, "they ought to have everyone stowed away in another hour and a half. Then the ships will leave fifteen minutes after that. We're getting there."

"All for the greater good," said Stan.

"All for the greater glory of the great god Leigh," said Nelson. The other overlords laughed.

"Eight years," said Denny. "They'll get there in eight years, all the craftsmanship and dedication that we could assemble. And they'll have nine years to absorb the best of what they find on Earth, to build a good home for themselves and for the poor unfortunates who left before them."

"You know," said Ed, making a drink for himself at the bar, "we're really very good at this."

"And we'll get better," said Chuck.

"We have a research team in Continent 3 that appears to be close to an even better propulsion system," said the delegate from that continent at the next meeting of Group Two.

"I'm glad to hear that," said the chairman. "I expected nothing less. When is this invention going to be made?"

The delegate consulted his notes. "We have it tentatively scheduled for the twenty-second of Septuary. It may happen the day before or the day after, but that's the general area."

"And has that team given you any idea how much better the system will be than the David Drive?" asked the chairman.

"Yes," said the delegate from Continent 3. "A fleet equipped with the new system will reach Earth in three years."

"What did our timetable call for?" said the chairman.

One of the recording secretaries searched through the thick notebook that was Group Two's timetable. He found the entry for this previously forecast invention. "About the twentieth of Septuary, a new propulsion system, reducing the journey to Earth to three point two five years," read the secretary.

"A couple of days off," said one of the other delegates, "but not bad."

"No," said the chairman, "we expected and planned for an even larger margin of error. The overlords will be pleased." There wasn't even a hint of doubt that on the predicted date the predicted invention would take place.

"There was a slackening in production following the expatriation of the craftsmen, farmers, and laborers," said the delegate from Continent 4. "This represented a reduction of our work force of about three-tenths of one percent. But we had previously planned for this, and the transition was made smoothly, and adjustments were made wherever necessary. Our population has been more than cooperative; the people have grown even more enthusiastic, as the project is delivering the milestone results it has promised. The slackening in production has been overcome, and already production is up nearly two percent, despite the loss of over a hundred thousand of our best farmers and workers. Those remaining have re-distributed the work load, and we're back on schedule."

"The schedule is all that counts," said the chairman.

The third fleet was smaller than the previous two hundred-ship fleets. There were only five ships in orbit around Jennings's World, equipped with the new Lenore Drive that would get them to Earth in slightly more than three years. The passengers they were destined to carry were the political officials, minor functionaries, and Group One itself, the overlords. These administrative personnel would make order out of Earth, so that when the fleet with the farmers, craftsmen, and laborers arrived, the world they found would be similar to that which they were called upon to abandon.

The overlords themselves had no qualms about leaving Jennings's World. As Nelson put it, "a planet is a planet." The overlords left Jennings's World under the care of a provisional military government, ruled jointly by General Melissa and General Jennifer.

Before they left for the shuttle craft that would lift them into orbit, the overlords gave one last televised address to their subjects. They sat in a semicircle, in comfortable captain's chairs, sipping drinks and appearing at ease. They were a little saddened at leaving the planet of their birth, but the prospects of the future excited them. They looked forward with eagerness to the challenges of Earth. Each of them, in turn, gave a speech. They went in the numerical order of their continents.

"When we arrive on Earth," said Tom, "we will find raw materials to work with. We will find these resources in metals, in fuels, and in the native talents of the people of Earth. All of these things will be exploited for the betterment of the people of Jennings's World. We have given up our privileges as overlords to insure this. We have broken ties with family and friends. We have guaranteed ourselves the impossibility of sharing in the benefits we will travel so far to secure for you. But we do all this gladly. Be sure that you will be forever in our thoughts."

The camera swung from Tom, who seemed to be wiping a tear from his cheek, to Chuck, who was swallowing a mouthful of liquor. He made a wry face, coughed, and then waved at the camera "Wait a minute," he said. He tried to speak, but he just started coughing again. Finally, the camera swung over to Stan.

Stan was adjusting his coat and the turtleneck sweater he wore under it. He scratched his stomach thoughtfully before he began speaking. "I really don't know what to say," he said finally. "This experience will be wonderful and terrifying. It is something that has to be done, so we are doing it. But we're not going alone. No, we're taking a little bit of each of you with us. And that is what makes the whole venture bearable. I guess that's all I have to say. Goodbye, and may the great god Leigh bless you all."

Denny was stifling a yawn when the camera pointed toward him. He laughed softly. "I just can't bring myself to be as serious as my colleagues. I think this is an occasion for celebration. We had a small party here, for our families and friends. As you can see, this isn't a formal state session. This is just your overlords, getting together for the last time on our world, wishing each and every one of you the very best, and may god bless."

From off-camera came Chuck's voice. "We have to leave in about five minutes," he said.

The camera turned to Ed. "Thanks," he said. "We're getting very near the end of our time with you, and the time we have left here on Jennings's World. It's been a good time, these last few years, and we have the great god Leigh, himself on his way toward Earth, to thank for all of that. I might only say that we have ourselves to thank as well, for as a potter is helpless without his clay, so too is a great god unable to perform his miracles without the rough materials that we provided for him. So we can look on the progress we have made and congratulate ourselves, and think of the coming promise of Earth as our reward. So have a good time, and think of us now and again. I'd like to say a special hello and goodbye to the people of Continent 5, who have worked so well to make my job so easy. Thanks, people, and flourish."

"And I thought that I was the pompous bureaucrat,"

said Nelson. Ed laughed, and Denny choked on the drink he was sipping. The camera turned to Nelson, who laughed. "I don't know what to say. I feel like Stan. I'll miss a lot of things. I'll miss that great little restaurant on the corner of Thirty-Sixth and Michael. But so what? General Melissa and General Jennifer will take care of you now, and I know that you'll keep working to improve our homeland. Perhaps some day we'll return, in our retirement. I don't know. We have to go. Good luck, and may the great god Leigh bless."

The televisions that carried the image of the overlords went blank. Old movies came on. The overlords went outside, where automobiles were waiting to take them to the shuttle craft.

Group Two met again, and once more predictions were made and trends cited. As in the previous stages of the project, it happened that the predictions were fulfilled with astounding accuracy. Eleven weeks after the overlords and their subordinates left Jennings's World, the most sophisticated propulsion system yet developed was announced by a research team from Continent 4. The Adele Drive would get a fleet of ships to Earth in a matter of weeks, not years. With a journey of only some twenty-four days, the passengers on board would not need to be put into suspended animation. A good deal of the fleet's packaged energy could be routed to other purposes, although food and other considerations for the conscious people balanced this new advantage.

A fleet of one hundred ships outfitted with the Adele Drive hovered over Jennings's World within a month of the propulsion system's invention. This was the final fleet, the last stage of Group Two's project. The timetable had been adhered to precisely, and there were only a very few more items left unaccomplished.

The world was searched in much the same manner as it had been combed for its best farmers and workers. Now, however, the search was for warriors. The fiercest and most ruthless men and women were called, assembled, and put through a two-week training period. They emerged an army, a disciplined, rugged force that easily might overwhelm any opposition that Earth could muster against it. To support this army, complex and murderous weapons systems were installed in the hundred ships. Earth would be attacked first from orbit, softened to the point of virtual capitulation, and then the army would land. The defenses of the victim world had been described in detail by the great god Leigh; Group Two estimated that few changes had been made on Earth in the years since Leigh's departure from that planet.

"It's a wonderful day for the departure of the army," said the television announcer. "The air is warm and fresh, and many thousands of spectators have gathered outside the Continent 1 spacecraft facility to watch the huge shuttle craft lift off at noon today. We'll be here right through—"

Alexei Engerev turned off the set and sat back down on his couch. There was a knock on one of the two doors that interconnected with the other apartment cells. It had to be Benarcek. Engerev looked up, and Justin Benarcek came into the room. "Were you watching?" he asked.

"Yes," said Engerev. "For a little while."

"What do you think?"

"What do you mean, what do I think? I think they're going to go to Earth and kill a lot of people we know. That's what I think."

Benarcek looked as though he were about to break down. He shook his head. For a moment. he was unable to speak. "And we can't do anything?" he asked finally.

"When have we ever been able to do anything?" said Engerev angrily. "Before we came to this damn planet or after."

Benarcek shook his head again. He did not answer.

Engerev stood up and went to the television. He turned it back on. The announcer was still chatting pleasantly. Engerev turned the sound off. "I wonder how many epics will come out of this," he said.

"I wonder if they're still worshipping Leigh," said Benarcek. "He's been gone a while. These people move so fast, I wonder if they'll go past him. Maybe they'll forget him or disprove him or something."

"I don't care."

"For our sake," said Benarcek "For Sanchito, and

Judy, and, God, poor Carolyn. God, Giacomo. I haven't even thought about her in months. It doesn't seem real, now. She was killed by a Bronze Age spear just a few years ago, and now these people are ready to blast off toward Earth. They have incredible things on those ships, you know."

"They can liquefy a city if they want to," muttered Engerev.

"That's what I mean. And I suppose we'll see it all, some day. Tapes of the whole thing. I bet they'll send a ship back with it."

"I won't see it," said Engerev, getting up and pacing the length of the room. His voice shook.

Benarcek responded instantly. "What do you mean?" he asked.

Engerev stopped his pacing for a moment and stared at his companion with a sullen expression. "What's wrong with you?" he asked. "Can't you figure anything out? Do you think I'm going to sit around this room for the next thirty years or so? Or wait until they want to use me, like they used Sanchito?"

"You can't kill yourself," said Benarcek, horrified.

The astrogator laughed briefly. "Why not? I'll give you odds that I can."

"We're the only two left," said Benarcek. "We're all that Earth has here. We owe it to our people to stay alive, keep hoping."

Engerev snorted scornfully. "Don't you see?" he asked. "It's our fault! It's all our fault!"

Benarcek just stared, his mouth open. The Russian started pacing again. Benarcek wept quietly. Neither of them said anything more for a long while.

The army of Jennings's World appeared suddenly, the hundred ships popping into existence near Earth and taking their offensive positions before the space fleet of Earth could react. Warnings were broadcast, and then the warships of Jennings's World began their terrible destruction. They did not cease for five days, and by then Earth was pleading for clemency. The shuttle craft transported the army to the surface of the blue planet; the army of Jennings's World met with no resistance. They operated more as police, keeping order, than as an advancing army.

The loose governments and organizations of Earth had disappeared. The feeling of community which had brought the peoples of Earth together was at first strengthened by the threat, and then desroyed. There were only individuals, couples, family groups, trying to stay alive and stay together. The army of Jennings's World took control, and the officers imposed martial law. Gradually, life returned to a more normal manner, although a strange version of anything anyone on Earth had ever known. It was life in the midst of ruin, life under the rule of an incomprehensible conqueror. It was many weeks before the people of Earth even understood where their new masters had come from. Then, even then, only a few people connected the army of Jennings's World with Project People to People. It was an irony that was shared by few and enjoyed by even fewer.

When the overlords arrived some three years later, they found a world that was being operated in a merciless, militarily efficient way. This is what they expected. They were very pleased.

"Well," said Tom, "this is indeed very pleasant. The timetable seems to have been successful. Group Two deserves a reward. I'm sure they've taken it."

"Speaking of that," said Ed, "how are we going to split up the continents?"

"Do you want to do that now?" asked Chuck. "We just got here."

"Let's get it over with," said Stan.

"All right," said Chuck. They all put their names on slips of paper, and put these in a shoe. Then one of their advisers picked slips out. The first choice belonged to Tom.

"North America," he said.

"Damn," said Stan. "I wanted that."

"Chuck," said the adviser.

"Europe," said Chuck."

Denny took Asia, Ed took Africa, Nelson took South America, and Stan was left with the Pacific area, made up of Australia, Japan, and the islands in between.

"Let's go introduce ourselves," said Ed.

"Great," said Nelson. "I have plans to make first, though."

"I've already made a few," said Tom. "I can't wait until Leigh gets here. He's not so special, any more."

Denny looked thoughtful. "Still," he said, "to our people who are already here in the army, and who will be coming later, he's the great god. We just can't make him a slave or something."

"And he'll be very unpopular with his own people," said Chuck.

"We'll think of something," said Tom, laughing. "We have—what?—fourteen years or so. We've got to raise the standard of living here. This place is worse than I expected."

"We've got plenty of time," said Chuck. They toasted each other with drinks which another adviser had brought them, and then they went out to meet their subjects. They had decided, from Leigh's talks, that they couldn't be overlords on Earth. The people of Earth cherished a fantasy of democracy and participational government. So the overlords decided to call themselves Representatives. The whole plan would evolve in the next few days, and they would go with what seemed right. They had had enough experience to trust their instincts in these matters. And there was no one to dispute them.

"All right, guys," said Tom, "let's hit the deck." They walked toward a waiting crowd of army officials from Jennings's World. Behind them were ranks of soldiers, men and women. Far, far behind these were the beaten people of Earth. It would be as close as they would ever get to their new Representatives.

PART ONE

1953

CHAPTER 11

On Earth, it was the year 1953. On Jennings's World, nearly seventy years before the arrival of the Project year 0 for another sixty-eight years. Nothing had ever always been the year 0, and it would continue to be the year 0 for another sixy-eight years. Nothing had ever happened on Jennings's World. It would be thirty-five years before the existence of Jennings's World would even be suspected. On the green world, humanoid creatures lived miserable lives, without warmth, with little food, with no sense of kinship or dignity. They were like people, but they were still animals.

Of what did their lives consist, then? Eating, finding food, keeping the food from the hands of the others who would steal it, finding more food, eating . . . Occasionally, a male and female would come together in mutual lust, and the race was perpetuated. There was nothing beyond these two simple routines. There was nothing more to distinguish these creatures.

They had learned to walk upright, giving them an advantage over other creatures who lived beneath the surface of a sea of grasses. But to make any kind of journey through the grass meant a constant, tiring brushing away of the grass, the irritating, maddening, wave upon wave of grass. To get water, the tribes made their way along animal paths; the humanoids never knew what kind of animals would be drinking along with them. Sometimes there were deerlike creatures, doglike creatures, large lizards. Sometimes there were great vicious cats lying in wait, and then, always, one of the unprotected humans died. Life had gone on like this for countless years. Nothing had happened yet to change it.

In one of the small groups of savages, living in a small grove of low, twisted trees, there was a boy. This boy was, by Earthly count, thirteen years old. He was in no way special or different from any other of his tribe or his race. He had never shown any special traits or aptitudes. There were no ways that speciality might be displayed. There was only food-gathering every day. The boy did well at that. He was never very hungry. He knew the best place to look for the swollen white root nodules that he could gnaw all morning. He knew of a patch of blue beans, and he was wise enough to keep that information secret. He went to the bean patch and ate; he never brought the beans back to the quiet grove that sheltered his tribe.

The idea of family had not yet been born. The boy didn't know who his father was or who his mother was. It was unlikely that his parents would have recognized or even understood that he was a product of their union. Too many years had passed since his infancy, too many meals had had to be found, too many things had been forgotten.

The boy was more active than the older men and women. He did not mind so much the stinging of the grass as it sprang back into his eyes while he walked through it. He started at a young age to explore the area around the grove. On one such exploration he discovered the blue bean patch. On another, he found a number of wild berry bushes. He ate well, while the primitives who chose to remain, more or less comfortably, in the grove had poorer meals. The boy was neither happy nor miserable. He did not suffer, except with the cold, and there was nothing that he could do about that except huddle closer to the others under the swaying boughs of the gnarled trees.

One morning, when hunger drove him out of the grove in search of a more satisfying meal than could be found among the trees, the boy saw a bird flap clumsily up from the weeds shortly ahead of him. The boy ran after it, although the bird quickly gained an advantage in altitude that the boy could not overcome. He grabbed at the bird, but of course with each second the bird flew further out of reach. Still the boy ran, even as the bird became nothing more than a soaring speck against the cloudy white sky. Finally, exhausted, the boy stopped. The grass that had bent in his passage sprang back up behind him. He was enclosed in a virtual prison of grass, unable to see anything but the rolling clouds overhead. The grass tickled his face, his eyes watered, but the boy just grimaced and continued. Unable to see any landmarks ahead or behind, he had no idea in what direction he was going. He was too uneducated, too inexperienced, too unobservant to notice that he was lost. To know that, he would have had to have a much more developed sense of his own identity, his relationship with his tribe, their particular domain, and the dull but secure life he had lived for thirteen years.

The boy walked through the grass, one hand held about a foot in front of his face, the other hand half that distance and a little lower. This was the best way to go through the grass, pushing it aside as one walked, forcing a narrow path. Nevertheless, a good deal of the grass still brushed him, irritated him. He ignored it. The only real danger from the terrain were sudden pits or half-buried boulders, invisible beneath the surface of the grass.

The boy marched through territory he had never traveled before, although he did not know it. It looked like grass, it looked like every other place he had ever seen, except the grove and the few islands of shrubbery and bushes that appeared unexpectedly in the ocean. It was a good day, not too cold, although the sky promised rain later. The boy was untroubled by any thoughts except finding food; he had always found it before, and he was confident that he could again. Finding food meant only looking long enough. If he pushed through the grass, even though it might take hours, he would come upon a patch of beans, or a bush of berries, or another grove that would supply gnawing roots, or even something completely new. It just took time, and the boy had no idea of time, no idea of hours or years; there was only light and darkness. One slept during darkness, but the boy, if he could speak,

167

could not have explained why. Why sleep during darkness? Because the sunlight kept one awake, of course.

The sun rose in the cloudy sky and shone a pale disc behind the white clouds. It moved overhead, and during its passage, the boy felt his hunger grow. It was a constant feeling, but it did not distress him. It was a day's hunger, and he had put up with quite a bit more in his young life. He did not let his mild discomfort slow him or distract him. In fact, it motivated him more to keep looking. The only guide he had was the sun, and he followed its path to prevent himself from traveling in circles.

After a while the grass thinned ahead and disappeared. The boy stumbled into a clearing. There was a space about ten yards square, covered with a thick, ivy-like growth a few inches above the ground. As he tried to walk through it, the boy found that the plant clung to his naked feet and ankles with uncountable stiff claws. He raised one painful foot, tearing it from the grasp of the ivy, and saw that it was bloody. He looked at the clearing filled with the plant; ahead was a shady and comfortable grove, empty of people, much like his own home grove. There, surely, was food. He stood there for another moment, one foot raised, while he puzzled out the situation wordlessly. Then, grimacing, he turned and ran back to the grass he had left. Each step was agonizing, as the ivy ripped at his flesh. He regained the comfort and safety of the grass. Both feet were sore and painful; hundreds of the ivy's sharp fingers were still imbedded in his flesh. He did not know what to do about that. Pain was something that happened occasionally; experience had taught him that it always went away. He shuddered and tried to ignore the hurt and spasms of aching that twinged through his feet and up his legs with every step.

The boy followed the grass around the clearing, staying near the edge so that he didn't stray too far. He turned a corner, still safely within the grass, and walked closer to the grove. A minute later, and he was gratefully within the shady confines of the trees.

It did not occur to the boy that this grove might be the home of another tribe, just like his. Imagination and insight are qualities that need to be developed and exercised before they can be called on with confidence. The boy and his tribe had little reason to use imagination. When the boy saw the grove, he recognized it merely for what it was: a stand of trees, of a sort different from the ones in which he resided. That was where his thinking stopped.

His next train of thought concerned locating food. He began to dig at the base of one of the trees, using only his strong fingers and short stubby fingernails to aid him. He had not yet discovered the use of tools, nor had any of his kinsmen. He dug painfully, for the ground was dry and hard. Slowly, though, he deepened and widened the hole until he saw the first sign of a root. He smiled. The tree's roots were inedible, of course, but if he followed the root far enough, it would lead to one of the nodules that nourished most of the members of his tribe. He was very hungry, and he worked harder now that his goal was in sight.

He used his forefingers and his middle fingers, held stiffly, to scrabble away at the dirt around the root. He dug deeper, as the root plunged deeper into the ground. He dug for a quarter of an hour without uncovering an edible nodule. He did not give up. Sometimes, he knew, one could follow a root for a foot or more before a nodule appeared. He dug for another half an hour, until the hole was nearly three feet deep, and he had uncovered a good deal of the root. There were no nodules. Wearily, the boy sat back against the bole of he tree. He looked upward, noticing again the strange, straight, smooth trunks of the trees, the wide, spatulate leaves that waved restlessly in the freshening breeze. These were not the same kind of trees that he was used to at home. Perhaps, the idea came, perhaps they did not have edible nodules at all. The notion was discouraging, but the boy shook off the feeling. There would be something else to eat. He stood up, feeling again the intense pain in his feet. The stiff briars of the ivy-like growth still stuck in his skin, and every step brought new agony. The boy ignored the pain for a moment, as he noticed that there were large nuts growing on the trees, about the size of his fist. He reached up to a limb that hung only a few inches above his head, plucked a nut, and sat down.

He could not bite the nut; it was much too hard. He

would have to break it open. He hit the nut against the ground. Nothing happened. He hit the nut against the bark of the tree. The bark shredded a little, and the nut made a small cracking sound. The boy continued to hit the nut until it split along a midline. Inside was a soft, sweet meat. The boy smiled; these were better than the blue beans or the berries, and they were more numerous.

While he sat, eating the nut, he began to pluck the ivy thorns from his feet. Each thorn left a sharp stinging, but the boy did not change expression. Pain was somethng that was quickly forgotten. In a while he had removed all of the ivy's protective growths, and his fingers and feet were covered with his blood. Then, slowly and painfully, he got to his feet and picked another nut. After a few seconds of banging it against the tree trunk, he had it, too, open.

While he made his meal on the nuts, the boy was unaware that something else was watching his movements with more than idle curiosity. Hidden in the grass at the edge of the clearing was a large, hungry grass cat, which sat watching the boy. Its coat was the same color as the grass, and it did not move while it observed the boy, not even a twitching of its long tail; that would have moved the grass in a telltale back and forth motion.

The cat was in the tall grass on a side of the ivy-clearing adjacent to the trees, not more than forty yards from the boy. It could creep another few feet closer, but then it would have to leave the shelter of the grass and charge across the broken ground of the grove. It waited and watched as the boy cracked another nut. The cat was hungry; it raised itself up slightly, gathered its paws beneath its huge, spare body, and leaped.

The rushing sound of the grasses parting made the boy look up. He saw the cat running from its sheltered position. He could see the fangs as the cat bared them in a low, desperate growl. The boy was paralyzed for a moment. This was not the first time that he had seen a grass cat, nor the first time that he had been charged by one. But he was out of his familiar territory. This was the cat's area, not his own. He got up and ran deeper into the grove. He cut left and right, making sharp turns around trees. He could have climbed one, but that would have made no difference to the determined grass cat. The boy could be eaten on a tree limb twenty-five feet above the ground as well as near the roots of the tree.

The boy was in good physical condition. His travels, his daily runs from danger, his pleasure in physical exercise all helped him now. It was the weaker members of the savage tribes, the ones who did not keep themselves fit, who died eventually beneath the claws and teeth of grass cats or other natural enemies.

The boy ran, as fast as the great, loping strides of his pursuer. The boy began to tire, but so did the cat. The cat tried to cut off the boy's path, but the boy just turned around and headed back the way he had come. The cat came around again, and the boy started in a different direction. The grove came to an end. Ahead was a small area of grass, and then a knoll that rose above the grasses like the decayed ruins of an ancient fortress. The boy headed for that, hoping to find a tiny cave in which he might safely hide. He ran up the side of the rocks, searching quickly. Nothing looked inviting. There were a few openings, but each was too large to protect him. The boy made a quick decision, sprang over the top of the knoll, and ran down the opposite side. He could hear the cat, a few seconds behind him, doing the same. The boy ran through the grass, and his own sound and the cat's merged in a gentle swishing. The boy ran back to the grove.

The cat came out of the grass and saw the boy running through the trees, still some yards ahead. The boy's breath began to come harder now; he was panting with the exertion. He made a couple of time-saving turns through the trees. Then he came to the one that he had examined earlier. Without slowing, he leaped for the low branch and swung out and up into it. The cat did not notice, but ran by, out of the grove, into the patch of viciously toothed ivy. The cat, snared by thousands of the plant's thorns, howled in rage. It rolled back and forth, each motion catching more of the ivy's teeth in the smooth fur. The boy could see the animal bleeding from innumerable wounds. The ivy, at least, would feed well this day. The boy looked down at his own tough, still aching feet. He shrugged. Then he swung down and edged around the clearing, through the grass, and back toward his own home. The grass cat did not seem to notice. The animal would have enough difficulty getting itself out alive before it weakened from loss of blood.

The boy followed his own slightly trampled path back home. It was not long before he saw mounds of rocks sticking above the grass that he recognized as landmarks. He stopped at the stream for a long drink of water; he was surprised that he did not meet any of his tribe there. Slowly, because he was tired, the boy headed for their stand of gnarled trees. He was still a little hungry; the nuts he had eaten had been good, but the cat had interrupted his meal. The boy would have to finish by digging for root nodules with the others that night. The nodules were becoming harder to find, also, for without them the trees died. It would not be long before the savage band would have to find another dwelling.

The boy came at last to the grove he had known as his home. He was astonished that not a single member of his tribe was there. Not even the oldest, most sickly men and women. All were gone, and all traces of them had gone, too, as though his tribe had never inhabited that particular copse. For a moment the boy was confused; he thought that perhaps he had, indeed, become lost, and had arrived at the wrong forest. But no, the trees were familiar themselves, and the holes dug at the roots. For some reason the entire community had gone elsewhere. The boy could not understand. He ran through the stand of gnarled trees, looking wildly from one side to another, hoping to discover someone, an ancient man or a young child, who had straggled away or been left behind. But he found no one in the entire stand of trees. He searched the grove from end to end, from side to side. He was alone.

The boy grew frightened, more frightened even than when he had been chased by the grass cat. Then, at least, the situation was a normal one, one that he could comprehend in his primitive, undeveloped mind. With the cat, it was life or death for one or the other. He ran, and the cat ran after him. Whoever ran the fastest or the most skillfully would survive. Today, it was the boy. At some future date, it would be the cat. But the situation that the

172

boy found in his home grove distressed him far more because nothing like it had ever happened in his experience. Never before had more than a couple of members of the community ventured forth from the protective shelter of the trees. Very few people wanted to. But now they were all gone, every single one of them. The boy stopped by a tree on the verge of the grove and stared out at the ocean of grass. He did not know what to do.

He thought that possibly they had all gone down to the stream for water; the idea was silly, but it offered an explanation. He discarded it however; he had just come from the stream and had seen no markings or footprints that would have shown that the tribe had been there together.

Perhaps, while the boy had been gone, the community had decided that the forest could no longer provide food for them all, and gone off to find another. The boy knew where the nearest likely groves were, and the only thing that he could think to do was search them. He took a deep breath; the sun was already falling in the west. He set out through the grass again.

As he approached another grove of trees about six hundred yards from his own, he became aware of strange, almost painful, noises in his head. He looked around for their source, but he saw nothing unusual. The noises cracked and spat like a thunderstorm in his head. He stopped, completely confused, afraid, and very lonely. If someone else had been with him, he would have felt more secure. But this was the first time that the boy had ever been abandoned. The noises in his head stopped for a moment. The boy shook his head. He dug his fingers in his ears. Then he continued on slowly through the grasses.

The sounds in his mind started again, louder, angrier, with a tone of threat that the boy could not understand. They were only sounds, and they were threatening him inside his own head. How could that be? He slowed even more, and as he crept forward he felt his throat and mouth go dry. Beneath the mad noises in his head he could hear the rapid, heavy beating of his heart. He was very afraid, but he knew that somehow all of this was the cause of his dilemma. He lay down in the grass and slowly pulled it away in front of him. Beyond was a clearing and a grove, just as he knew there would be. And the grove was filled with people and things.

Things. The things were like people, but they were much more horrible. They were tall and slender, with large black faces. They seemed to have long fangs, but the feature that drew the boy's attention was the eyes of the things. They were huge and golden, and they seemed to glow in the dimming light of dusk.

At one side of the grove a kind of pen or corral had been built. The boy forced his attention away from the black monsters to the pen, because inside it sat all the members of his tribe. They did not move. It was as if they were paralyzed or dead. Two of the black monsters guarded them. Another was raising and lowering his fist at the humans. It seemed to the boy that whenever the monster lowered his fist there was a sudden, loud crackle of noise in his head. After a time he began to realize that the monsters were communicating, or trying to, just the way that the boy and his tribe communicated by gestures and grunts and expressions. But the black monsters were sending noises inside the boy's head. The boy decided that the noises were supposed to mean something, but he had no way of knowing what.

slowly pulled it away in front of him. Beyond was a clear-

He sat silent for a moment, considering what to do. He gave no thought to the prospect of rescuing his tribe; that was impossible with all the black monsters standing around. That meant that the boy was truly alone in the world. What could he do? He could seek out another community of savages and try to be accepted as a member. But his mind brought up a memory of what had happened when a man had come to their community a few years before, alone and seeking food. He had been a stranger, and the savages had not trusted him. They had been afraid. They were always afraid of strangers. The man had been attacked and killed. And then he had been thrown out of the grove, as food for the grass cats so the animals would not attack the community for a few days. No, the boy decided, it would be impossible to try to join another community of humans. But did that mean that he was destined to be completely alone for the rest of his life? The boy's poor imagination balked at picturing such a situation, and he came back to thinking about the immediate situation. That was simpler. He had to get away from the black monsters.

The boy ran. Behind him he heard the whicking of the grass as he raced through it. He had no idea where he was going, but at the moment it did not seem to make very much difference. Then he heard the angry noises in his head. There were more, as though more than one of the black monsters was talking. The boy still couldn't understand what was being said, and the pain that accompanied the mindspeech was so great that tears almost blinded him. He turned to look back. He stood up as high as he could, and he saw three of the black monsters following him. They were so tall that the grass came only to their chests. Their dull, glowing golden eyes stared at him. The boy turned and ran in the direction of the old grove.

Then he heard the baying of the black monsters' hounds. It was a chilling sound, the sound of certain death if the hounds ever caught up with the boy. It was a vicious, hungry, murderous sound. The boy looked over his shoulder as he ran, but the monsters' hounds were hidden by the grass.

The monsters were some hundred yards behind. Their hounds were on long leashes; the boy knew that if the hounds were loosed, his life would very likely be over in a matter of seconds. But a flash of insight told him that the black monsters didn't want him dead. They wanted him captured, like the rest of his tribe. In that case, he had the chance to outrun them. He wondered if he could hide from them. After all, when he hid from one of the members of his tribe he sometimes sneezed or grunted, and was thus discovered. And if the black monsters were able to force their grunts inside his head, perhaps they could listen there, too. The boy grimaced. He would have to take the chance. He ran, his feet bleeding and painful. His legs were nearing their threshold of exhaustion, and his chest hurt as he gulped air.

His idea was to race for the knoll he had discovered while he was being chased by the grass cat. Perhaps he could hole up in one of the rock fishers. He pictured himself there, hiding in one of the shallow crevices, his eyes tightly shut, his mouth closed, his breathing quiet and slow. Unless these black monsters and their unseen but terrifying hounds had special powers, the boy felt that he could remain safely in the rocks until they went away. He wished that he knew what they wanted and how long they were going to stay. Did they intend to kill his tribe? Did they want to capture him only to kill him? Then why not unleash the hounds?

The low, wavering howl of the hounds sounded closer than ever. With a sudden shudder of fear, the boy realized that some of the noise was coming from his right, and there seemed to be a hound coming from directly in front. They had encircled him. He turned to his left, giving up the plan to run for the rocky knoll. There were black monsters in every direction but to the left. He ran for his freedom.

After a few minutes, there was a frightening howl ahead of him. The boy jumped a little, to see over the top of the grass; there, not more than forty yards away, was the evil face of one of the tall black monsters. The boy heard another hound behind him, and one coming from the right. He turned again. This procedure continued until, after some time, the boy saw that he was being herded toward the corral in which the rest of his tribe was confined. It seemed that whatever their fate, he would join them.

"Go," came the noise in his head. It meant nothing to the boy. "Go." The black monster repeated the order, again and again. It was the first word the boy ever heard, and the first word he learned. *Go*. In a few minutes, he was corraled with his tribe. No one greeted him. Everyone sat, eyes blank, expressions showing nothing. None of the savages knew what was happening.

The boy sat down, too. He waited, glad of the chance to rest from the running, glad to let his bleeding feet rest as he lay back in the grass.

"Go," came the call again, and the boy saw that every head in the corral jerked. They had all learned the word well. The primitives stood; the boy sighed. His respite had been short. One of the black monsters spoke to them in their minds, but no one understood what he said. "Go," he said at last, and the humans docilely lined up by the opening to the corral. They were herded a short distance from the corral, into an open space which had been cleared of grass. The monsters went from person to person, finally choosing six. The boy was one of these. The six who were chosen were given shovels. "Dig," said one of the monsters in their minds. They did not understand the word. "Dig," repeated the monster. The savages just stood, looking confused. The monster took a shovel and started to dig with it. Then he gave it back to the human. "Dig," said the monster, and the human did just what the monster had shown him. The other five dug where the monsters indicated. This was the second word the humans learned.

They dug until the boy's hands were as sore and bleeding as his feet were. The holes were about five feet deep. When the monsters inspected the holes and decided that they were acceptable, another monster came with metal poles. These were placed in the holes and partially buried. The monsters pantomimed the work they wanted done, and the humans, quick to learn, performed the labor.

Six poles stuck up out of the ground. The monsters demonstrated how reinforcing sections were to be attached, using magnetic locks. Crossbeams were added, and more vertical poles, and the structure grew slowly. The humans learned their tasks quickly, and the crossbeams and the vertical poles were attached efficiently. A tall, tapering tower took shape high above the tops of the gnarled trees and the waving grasses. When the monsters judged that the tower was complete, they ordered the humans down. By this time the humans were repeating aloud whole sentences they had heard in their minds. They were assimilating the language of the black monsters.

One of the black monsters climbed the tower, carrying a radio package. The humans stared at the monster as he climbed higher and higher into the tower. The monster worked for many minutes installing the radio apparatus. Wires trailed down from his height, and other black monsters on the ground did various things with these wires. After a time, the monster in the tower signaled that he had completed his work. The words crackled in the minds of the humans, who were already beginning to understand more and more about the situation. They had already comprehended that they had been captured by the black monsters; this marked a sudden sophistication in outlook that the black monsters did not expect. It surprised them, and it pleased them, too. If these filthy, naked brutes were to become good slaves for the black lords, then a native though submerged intelligence might be a worthwhile attribute to cultivate. Of course, they knew from experience, it could be deadly as well.

When the black monster on the tower indicated that he had finished, he waited until another of his species checked the results with some complicated electronic equipment. "It looks good," thought the monster on the ground. "It's broadcasting. We'll find this lump of world whenever we need to." The monster in the tower began to descend, and the human primitives around the base of the tower tried to decipher what the monster had meant. The intellectual content of the words was still beyond them, although only the word "broadcasting" was unfamiliar to them now.

When the black monsters had closed their ranks, they began giving orders to the humans in the sharp, painful mindspeech. "Go," ordered the monsters, and the humans understood well enough. They followed a black monster who held one of the hounds on a leash. The beast, which the boy saw for the first time, was more of a nightmare than anything he had ever seen. It appeared to be nothing more than a huge torso supported by rows and rows of rippling legs, giant, bloodied claws, and a head that was mostly yellow teeth. Its giant eyes glowed, just as its master's did, but the color was a ghastly, deathly shade of blue. The humans followed in close order until they arrived at the landing craft of the black monsters.

"Go," ordered the first monster, holding his hunting hound back from attacking the attractive bits of meat that were the primitive humans. The savages knew at once now that the black monsters wanted them to board the landing craft. Suddenly, with a newly developed sense of what was being done to them, they were afraid. They knew that boarding the craft would be the end of their lives as they had lived them, century after century, generation after generation. They knew that they would never see their grove again, or the rippling waves of grass.

Something irrevocable would be done by entering the landing craft. But the black monsters represented power, and their hunting hounds were fierce enough to enforce any order. The humans were thrown aboard and marched to the rear, where they found themselves in a rather bare hold, furnished only with wooden racks padded with thin mattresses to guard minimally against the forces of acceleration.

The humans were left alone in that section of the landing craft. After about ten minutes, a loud siren sounded in the ship. The humans, startled, sat up in wonder. They had no idea of what to expect. Then the rocket engines began firing, and the primitive humans huddled against the walls of the hold, clinging to each other in their fear and coldness. The landing craft climbed into the air slowly, rising vertically from the surface of what would be, in several decades, Jennings's World. Then the craft tilted until its front end pointed into the sky, and the rockets pointed back at the ground. The rocket engines were opened to full thrust, and the landing craft screamed into the sky. The humans were thrown all about the hold. The platforms they rested on had safety belts, but none of the passengers had any idea of their use. Many humans were dashed to death against bulkheads. Others were severely injured. The boy clung to a post until the muscles in his arms felt they could hold on no longer. Then the acceleration stopped, abruptly, and the bewildered humans were thrown into a weightless condition. From ports in the sides of the ship they could look down and see their green world, but no one had any idea of what it was. They had not understood that they had traveled into the sky, and that the lovely green ball that hung below them was their former home.

For some time the shuttle craft seemed to fall through space. Those of the humans who were still alive suffered from space sickness, a complete disorientation, and a constant and consuming terror.

Finally, the landing craft docked with the mother ship which orbited in a stationary position over one of Jennings's World's poles. From the ports, the primitive humans could look down and see the small cap of snow. Because of the tilt of the planet, the seasons did not change radically, and it was not often that the boy and his tribe experienced snow in his latitude—his former latitude, for the boy and his kinsmen were destined never again to set foot upon the world of their birth.

Many hours later, a black monster appeared through a hatchway with many squeeze packages of thin, hot stew. "Eat," he said in the harsh mindspeech. This was a new word, but hunger and the packages of stew soon made its meaning clear. Those who could stand the idea of eating while weightless fought their way toward the floating packages. Even among these hardy people, many who ate their portion vomited it up again. The stew was held in the packages by means of a thin membrane, through which steam and odor were permeable; unfortunately, when one of the humans vomited, it hung in the air, slowly dispersing in even, random movement toward the walls. Only the boy and a few other people were able to eat and keep the food in their stomachs. After eating, the boy was somewhat depressed. His body still ached and stung, and he lay back on one of the mattresses and slept. Even with all that had happened in the last few hours, he knew that his body needed rest to restore itself.

In the days that followed, the black monsters appeared again and again. As on the planet below the day of their arrival, the black monsters assumed the roles of taskmasters. The human savages had been taken as slaves. Evidently the black creatures considered them to be prime slave material, for the beacon had been raised to guide other slave-seeking missions to Jennings's World.

In the next few months, the ship of the black monsters traveled the dark reaches of interstellar space. They left behind Jennings's World, they left behind the star that scientists on Earth would identify as Wolf 359. They left behind the entire sector of space, on some important but undisclosed mission of their own. The boy learned to live in weightlessness. He learned to express himself in the language of the black monsters, although he had no success in reproducing the mindspeech of the aliens. He fashioned garments for himself, using material from the mattresses in the hold, in imitation of the black robes worn by the monsters. The other humans followed the boy's lead, each deriving new ideas and concepts which were eagerly discussed among the former savages. When the black monsters checked on their slaves a few weeks after takeoff, they were amazed that the human primitives had become semi-civilized creatures, with a family and social structure that had not existed when the black monsters had landed on Jennings's World. The black monsters were not overly curious; their ideas did not extend to a sociological examination of the inferior races they took as slaves. If the humanoids decided to improve their evolutionary standard, then that meant only better service to the black masters.

One of the important things that did happen, however, was that certain of the black masters, desirous of choosing their own private slaves, were interested in the change in the naked, filthy humans. Personality traits had appeared, taken over by the humans from the black monsters. The more astute of the black monsters realized that the better developed slaves would make admirable personal servants. In this way, the boy was chosen from his fellows to be the personal valet of one of the powerful black monsters. The boy did not care. It was a better life than that in the hold. The food was better, the clothing better, and the opportunity to learn was unexcelled. During the first few months, the boy absorbed everything he could about the culture of the black masters. He learned to speak well, he learned to read, and he learned to live by the hard, cold standards of the black monsters. But never, never did the boy become comfortable in the presence of the creatures and their glowing, baleful golden eyes.

At first, the boy's duties for his new master were simple. Every day he went to the area of the huge interstellar craft where the black monsters kept pens of small, green, lizardlike animals. The boy chose one, killed it, cut its head off, skinned and gutted it, and brought the remainder to his master for the black monster's daily meal.

The boy also wrote in a journal whatever his master dictated, as it appeared that the black creature was a historian or sociologist. In this way, the boy learned more about the language and the customs of the race of slavers that had captured him and his tribe. By this time, the boy was fully conversant with the written and spoken idioms of the language of the black monsters; after a while, he began teaching bits of it to the humans he chanced to meet during the day.

The other humans had less pleasant chores. They were often sent outside the ship to repair operational malfunctions. Whenever this happened, the unlucky people chosen to perform the task died. The black monsters preferred to suit the humans up in cheap, shoddy spacesuits with a limited amount of oxygen. Rather than wasting air by flushing it out with the people, the black creatures just left the humans outside to die of suffocation. Other humans performed menial tasks, were used in medical experiments or, sometimes, were eaten.

It was impossible for the boy to observe all of this without developing a deep hatred for the race of black monsters. They were hateful enough, just in appearance and manner. But the first time that the boy learned that the black monsters occasionally used the human slaves as food, he felt suddenly sick. This was an attitude that had developed since his capture; surely, before, on Jennings's World, he would not have been sickened to see any animal kill and eat any of his friends or fellows. Now, though, possibly through the vague and alien kind of education he had picked up through his acquaintance with his black master, he was appalled to hear what some of the fierce, evil creatures did. It wasn't every black monster that used the humans for food; the boy's own master was against that practice, as he set forth in his writings. Nevertheless, the boy had difficulty separating his feelings for the race of golden-eyed devils and those black creatures as individuals. His master was less cruel, but the boy had to admit that he hated his master as much as any of the other black monsters. The hatred grew in the boy as the months passed, and as the boy became more sophisticated in his learning and his habits. He clung to the simple ways he had known as an unenlightened savage; he did not need much food and he yearned for no luxuries. From this position, he could genuinely hate the black monsters with a cold passion.

It was some time before the boy realized what had happened. He had to go along, taking his education as he could, learning more and more about the habits and customs of the black race. But gradually the true picture filled in. The black monsters had come to Jennings's World on a mission of discovery and exploration. To their surprise and delight they found an indigenous race of humanoids who could be taken for slaves. The black monsters' economy was dependent on slave labor. So the creatures had captured as many of the humans as they could, and erected a radio beacon to lead other ships of the black monsters' fleet to the world for future raids.

The boy realized that his people, left on the planet, still in a prehistoric condition, unable to warm or feed themselves adequately, would be easy prey for the black monsters forever and ever. The boy's master was debating the ethics of this in his book. It was purely argumentative in nature; the boy's master had no doubts about the morality of taking these slaves. He was just idly setting up a hypothetical evil and then showing how such a *hypothetical* evil must be tolerated for the good of all. Never for a moment did the creature consider that the evil was more than merely conjectural. The boy tried a few times to argue with his master, but these attempts only ended in his being beaten.

Day after day, the boy saw members of his tribe die. He watched as a human in a spacesuit, out beyond one of the port windows, hanging from one of the spacecraft's long antennas, was cut loose rather than brought back inside. The boy felt his stomach tighten and his throat go dry as he watched the human floating farther and farther from the ship, paralleling its course but falling behind gradually. The human's arms and legs flailed for a few moments, then stopped. The boy watched until the odd movements of the human pushed it out of sight. Then the boy turned and went back to his quarters.

One day, as the boy was running an errand for his master, he walked down a corridor. Two humans were washing the walls and the floors. One of the black monsters came by in the opposite direction. The two humans working and the boy all stopped respectfully to let the black monster by. The creature inspected the walls which the humans were washing and declared that one human was doing a better job than the other. The black monster took out a long knife from his belt and cut open the abdomen of the inferior workman. Then he told the other human to clean up the mess.

The black monsters had other slaves, of course, besides the humans. There were examples of dozens of different species on the ship, all kept segregated by type until the individuals grew used to the condition of slavery. The black monsters never thought anything of killing a slave; they could replace slaves much more easily than they could take on fuel or food. There were uncountable planets in this sector of space where slaves might be taken. Indeed, the chief argument against the killing of slaves was only the need to land to replenish the work force. These repeated landings increased the cost of each spaceflight and lowered profits. But the idea of a slave as an article of some value, however small, was entirely foreign to the black monsters.

The boy determined that he was going to do something to help change the ideas of his owners. He didn't know where to begin, but he suspected the simplest thing might be to try to reason with his master. Although that had always failed in the past, the black monster often sat, staring with those dreamful golden eyes, while the boy tried to express what he felt for the plight of his fellow slaves. The master always ended up shaking his head, reaching for a heavy rod in a corner, and beating the boy until the boy was unconscious. This did not discourage the boy from trying to get through to his master.

At last the black monster decided that his slave was incorrigible and traded the boy for another, more docile, silent slave. The boy was put to work on another assignment; he realized that he could end up dead now, as he had seen others die. He worked hard. He was charged with stocking and checking the stores in various areas of the spacecraft. He came to know the general layout of the ship well. That was what gave the boy—now, by this time, no longer a boy, but a young man—his first great idea.

Whenever the boy was assigned to one of the landing craft, he was supposed to run through a detailed checklist of items, making sure that the emergency vehicle was properly supplied in case of need. But the boy always took a little extra time, using his superior education to read and study the mechanics of the landing craft. He did not know what exactly he was preparing for, but he had come to value any knowledge for its own sake, and he believed that if ever he could improve his lot—and the position of all the other slaves as well—he would have to know more about the black monsters and their methods of operation.

One day the youth was finishing up a checkout of one of the starboard-side landing craft. It looked to him to be the very one in which he had been lifted off Jennings's World to this spacecraft, to this life of slavery and knowledge, to the odd mixture of freedom and expression.

The more he looked around, the more certain he was that the landing craft was the same as that in which he was first captured. He stopped his work for a moment, thinking back to that day. It wasn't really very long ago; still, so much had happened in the meantime, he had learned so much. He had seen so much that he wished he hadn't. He felt an anger and a hatred rise in him. He thought about his former master, who had taught him to read and speak and write. The black monster was better than many, but he was still a towering, golden-eyed demon who would kill a slave as soon as argue with one. Almost before the youth knew what he was doing, he had pressed the emergency cutoff panel. A metal plate slid across the door, sealing the landing craft off from the mother ship. The youth stared at it in silence for a few seconds, frightened. If the black monsters caught him now, he was dead for sure. He continued to initiate the escape sequence. He checked the metered amounts of fuel, food, water, oxygen, and other consumables. They were all correct—he had taken care of that himself. A siren sounded outside, warning the ship that the shuttle was about to separate itself from the main craft. With a soft hiss the landing ship slid away from the black monsters' spaceship. The masters showed no sign that they cared; they probably didn't. A beam of light shot out from the front of the main craft, but the beam didn't intersect the path of the shuttle craft. The youth wondered if the beam of light might be a weapon firing. There was no way of knowing for sure. After that first beam, there were no more. The black monsters probably felt that whoever was inside the shuttle would soon be dead, and the effort to recapture a landing craft was too great for the prize. The shuttle went off in one direction in space, and the mother ship continued on, unperturbed.

The youth was terrified, when he realized what he had so carelessly done. He was alone, more alone than anyone had ever been. He was like the human in the spacesuit, cut off and floating away from the life of the mother ship. The youth had food, water, and fuel—how much? He did some quick computations. The shuttle craft had enough fuel for forty years of flight, thanks to the efficient engines of the black monsters. But food and water would be exhausted in a year and a half. So the youth sat down and thought. He had come from a world where he had lived a meager but successful life. And the black monsters had many kinds of slaves from many different worlds. Perhaps the youth could replenish his supplies as he traveled, until he found a hospitable world. He wondered if he could find his way back to his own home planet. He doubted that, for he had been given an idea of how vast the galaxy was. He sat quietly for some time. Then he made himself a large and filling meal, slept, and then began plotting his position using the astrometric equipment aboard the craft. He changed course for the nearest likely star system.

Years passed. More years passed for the boy, the youth, the man in the shuttle craft than he had lived on his own world. He traveled the stars as no one before him ever had—alone. He visited worlds where there were races of intelligent people, some of which he recognized from the slave pool of the black monsters. He stopped on worlds that were populated by abundant animal and vegetable growths, and no intelligent life forms at all to disturb things. He took on food and water, and he traveled.

Once, some twenty years after he had escaped from the ship of the golden-eyed slavers, he heard something. He had never heard anything aboard his shuttle craft before, other than the noises of the equipment and the noises he made himself. This was different, though. This was from outside. It was a voice. It wasn't like the voices of the black monsters, who spoke to one inside one's

186

head. This was a voice like the man's own people, made up of grunts and whistles and clicks. It was coming over the broadcast receiver. It was the first time anything had ever been picked up by the radio. The man knew at once that it meant intelligence. At first he was frightened. He listened. Soon words began to become differentiated. The man's quickness of mind began piecing together the grammar of the strange language. He guessed at the meaning of some of the more common words, and worked from there.

The man turned the outside radio antennas around to pull in the transmission as clearly as possible. He plotted the approximate location of the source of the broadcast. He searched the star maps of the shuttle craft and found that there was, indeed, a solar system in the general area of the broadcast. The man was excited. This was what he had hoped and prayed for throughout the twenty years of lonely exile he had passed aboard the landing craft. He scrapped the program that would have set him down on the nearest planet for a food and water stop. He estimated that he had more than enough food and water to make it to this world, where men spoke through space, and where he might be welcomed as something other than a hopeless slave.

The man sat down excitedly. He drew a circle around the star toward which the shuttle craft was now aimed. According to the star maps of the black monsters, there were no planets reported for that particular star, but the man knew that the black monsters had not mapped this region of the galaxy very well. It would take several months to reach his destination, and the man could hardly bear the suspense and the anguish of waiting. He listened to the radio all day, all night. He heard many different kinds of transmissions, and after a while he realized that they were coming in different languages. Different languages—from the same world! He wished that there were some way of shortening the journey. He spent as much time as he could listening to the broadcasts and transcribing them in the alphabet of the black monsters. He studied the languages until he was able to speak three or four of the most common.

The craft hurtled closer and closer to its goal, and

the man inside went nearly insane with anticipation. He had not thought about what his life would be like; never, when he had been an ignorant savage on his own world, did it seem important. When he had been a slave on the ship of the black monsters, *that* and only that had been his life, and it seemed that it would remain that way until one of the brutes killed him for some vague reason. Then, in the twenty years he had sailed the black seas of space, that had seemed to be what his life was all about. But now he had more of a purpose, although just what that purpose was was still clouded in his mind.

He listened to the radio, he plotted his course, he made tiny, fussy adjustments, he ate, he exercised, he slept, he paced the roomy confines of the shuttle craft. He could do nothing more. He didn't dare try to broadcast to the world he was approaching. He didn't know what kind of a reception he could expect; what he had learned from the transmission was that the people on the world were in some respects a lot like the black monsters: they killed often, and for only the sketchiest reasons. He didn't want to land on that world announced. He would make his presence known in his own time, when he thought it best.

He orbited the world, looking down at its lovely blue and white swirls. Orange and green continents flashed among the clouds. From down there came a rich and confusing mixture of broadcasts, so many that the man had to tune his radio finely to get the ones he wanted to study. He prepared himself. He had not been detected in orbit, or at least, if he had been, he had not been hailed. That indicated something about the technological level of the inhabitants. It was clear to the man that these people were nowhere near the level of the black monsters. That was fine with him. He had had enough of cold, bloodless, murderous genius. He wanted to learn other things, things no one he had ever known had been able to teach him. He knew from the radio broadcasts that these people valued things which the man could not even grasp. The density of conflicting ideas was intoxicating to him. He sat in orbit for a day and a night, making his plans. He picked out the major nations from listening to many days of radio broadcasts. He located them on the globe that spun slowly beneath him. He chose his landing site with great care—a lot depended on the way he was received. When everything was prepared to his liking, he began his descent.

The shuttle craft landed in a remote area far from a large city. He did not want to attract attention to his arrival from space. He knew enough about these people to know that that would frighten and alienate them from the beginning. He would have to pose as one of them for a while. He had to assume a cover identity, and slowly, slowly, build up the history that provided the solid facts of his life. He would have to obtain identification cards, he would have to forge and steal certain other things, but none of that bothered him. He had time. He had learned a lot from the black monsters. He would build himself a life on the world he had chosen.

While he waited for morning, he listened to a radio broadcast from a station nearby. "This is Bob Dunne, station KJNG, here in Jennings, Louisiana. I've got a request for Donna Fargo's new single for Bob McElroy and Lon Duclaire, driving to Houston tonight. Okay, Bob and Lon, here it is." The disc jockey played the song, then interrupted the last few seconds to announce again that the station was KJNG, in Jennings, Louisiana.

"Jennings, Louisiana," said the man in the space shuttle. Jennings, Louisiana."

Toward dawn he started walking, completely naked, along a highway. It was not long before he was picked up and taken to a police station. From there he was taken to a hospital. He told the people there that he didn't know how he came to be wandering the roads naked and alone. He seemed to be in a state of shock. When they asked him his name, he started in surprise. He had never had a name before. "Jennings," he said, thinking of the town the disc jockey had kept repeating. That's all that he would tell them, other than that he was "with the sky." The hospital employees assumed that he meant he was an astronomer. The man, now named Jennings, promised himself as he lay in the ward that somehow, some way, he would return to his home world and lead his savage brothers to a life this wonderful. The year was 1976. He had twelve years in which to extend "Jennings" into "Robert L. Jennings, Jr., and "with the sky" into Administrative Director of the New Orleans Center for Coordinated Astrometrics." And though he never saw his home world again, he kept his promise to his savage brothers.

GREAT SCIENCE FICTION FROM
WARNER BOOKS!